I DREAM OF MURDER

Catherine Dexter

Morrow Junior Books • New York

Printed in the United States of America.

1   2   3   4   5   6   7   8   9   10

Library of Congress Cataloging-in-Publication Data
Dexter, Catherine.
I dream of murder/Catherine Dexter.
p. cm.
Summary: Fourteen-year-old Jere is haunted by a recurring dream about a
murder he may have witnessed ten years earlier.
ISBN 0-688-13182-4
[1. Dreams—Fiction.   2. Nightmares—Fiction.   3. Mystery and detective
stories.]   I. Title.   PZ7.D5387Iae 1997   [Fic]—dc20   96-29346   CIP AC

For Anna, who loves mysteries

My thanks to Officer Bridget Kaskeski, of the Boston Police Department, Area E-5, and to Ed O'Brien, of the Franklin Park Zoo in Boston, for their help in the early stages of writing this book.

Chapter ONE

*S*omeone lay on the grass, and the man looked up and saw Jere. Jere was watching him from higher up. For several slow seconds, he and the man looked straight at each other. Jere was sitting on his ridey horse by his bedroom window and he was all alone in his room and he was afraid to move. He didn't want the man to see him; it felt as though his eyes were coming right through Jere's window, looking right into Jere's inmost self, as if he knew everything that Jere knew. The man had just done something bad, and Jere wasn't supposed to see it. He had already seen it, though—it was too late not to see it—and now it was running through his head like witches chanting. It had come right into him, what he had seen. Someone lay on the dark grass, where the man had hurt her.

"Are you about ready?" Jere's mother called through the door. "Your father's waiting in the car." Jere sat up, looked at his clock, jumped out of bed, and began tearing off his pajamas. His mother had come up earlier, he vaguely remembered; he must have gone right back to sleep. He pulled back the shade at his window. The sky was totally blue; long rays of sun fell through the trees in the park across the street. Perfect soccer weather.

"Jeremiah!" his mother called out. That was his real name, had been his grandfather's name, but everyone called him Jere—pronounced Jerry—except on ceremonial occasions or when they were really fed up. "Jeremiah Tucker Robison," his eighth-grade principal had intoned as he handed him his diploma. His grandfather had called himself Jere, too.

He was dressed in ninety seconds, running down the stairs in his stocking feet. He felt about as ready to play as a bag of wet sand. While he was gulping down some breakfast, he caught the edge of his cereal bowl with his elbow and the whole thing spilled down the front of his soccer shirt. His mother handed him a towel and his water bottle, and he raced out to the car, dabbing at his shirt. He jumped into the front seat. His mother got into the backseat.

"You both coming?" he asked his parents, trying not to sound dismayed. He actually liked it better when they didn't watch him play. His father went into his office nearly every Saturday, and lots of Sundays, too.

When he did come to a game, it was embarrassing. He looked very lawyerish with his crisp white shirt and his coat and tie, and he yelled too loudly. His mother taught at a law school, and she didn't usually have to work on weekends, so she came to most of his games. She was too dressed up, too, but Jere didn't mind so much with her. She looked nice in her blazer, and at least she wore jeans. She was as tall as Jere's father and had red hair that had been turning gray for quite a while. She was friendly with the other soccer parents, even though she said she was older than a lot of them.

Anyway, when they both came, they paid too much attention. If he screwed anything up, which he did often enough, they would go on and on afterward about how it was okay and he shouldn't feel bad. Which made him feel worse.

He bent down to tie his cleats, pulled too hard, broke a lace.

"Do you have any extras?" asked his father.

"Nope, not with me."

"Let's get some then."

"But I'm already late!"

His father turned three blocks out of the way and stopped in front of a big Valu-Mart. His mother ran in, then came out with a pair of neon green laces.

"Sorry. That's all they had," she said, handing them to him.

The stop made him even later getting to the field. He threaded the thing into his shoe, and everybody turned around to watch as he trotted out with a big wet place on the front of his shirt and one green shoelace glowing in the sun.

Things didn't improve much during the game. He couldn't seem to make his feet move on the grass; he never made it to the ball. Each time it hurtled by his part of the field, a herd of legs in black socks closed around it, someone's foot made contact, and the herd of legs chased on. He was so slow. He'd gotten taller over the summer, and his mother said he hadn't caught up with himself yet, but he was pretty sure that wasn't it. He knew the coach would play him less and less if he didn't start hustling. They were hoping to get to the Massachusetts state finals this year, so if you didn't play your best, you didn't get put in.

But his team won, and things started looking up. Lots of triumphant hoots and warbles. A bunch of the best players went off together in someone's beat-up old family van. Jere high-fived with the next-best players and slid into the backseat of his father's expensive car, knocking his knee against the door latch. He managed not to yell, "Ouch."

"Not bad, not bad," said his father as he started the car. "By the way, watch the mud back there."

"I'm watching it," said Jere, lifting one foot. Several lumps of clay fell off. Jere's father kept his car immaculately clean. It even smelled clean—leather seats and vacuumed carpets. "I'm going over to Avery's this afternoon, okay?"

"Oh, Avery," said his mother. "Do you have plans?" His mother kept an eye on his friendship with Avery. Now that Jere was in high school, she was trying, he could tell, to keep from prying into things that were his business, but she couldn't help asking about Avery. Probably anyone would. Avery was fourteen, like Jere, but she seemed older. She was pretty—better-looking for a girl than Jere was for a boy. By far. She was small and slender, with sleek black hair and hazel eyes and a sharp face. Jere had red hair like his mother and big feet like his father and was probably going to be tall, but he wasn't yet. Everyone knew he got good grades and behaved himself in school, which amounted to a distinct social handicap. Avery was a flake. People liked her— she was one of the popular girls—but she kept a certain wacky distance from everybody. She was pretty enough to get away with that.

"Jere, do you have plans?" His mother turned around and repeated her question.

"We're going to the zoo. We went a couple times last summer, remember?"

"That sounds nice."

Last spring, right before eighth-grade graduation, Jere and Avery had gone to the zoo one afternoon as a joke. It was Jere's idea. Avery said she had never been to the city zoo, so he said why didn't they pretend they were little kids again and go. By then, they had been friends for half the year, and Jere was pretty much over thinking that she would dump him any day. They took the bus to the Metropolitan Zoological Park and spent a couple of hours going through the African Rain Forest House and the outdoor "free flight" birdcage. They watched two shaggy camels slowly walk with drooping ankles across a straw-littered yard. A fat zebra switched its tail in the shade of a tree, its black-and-white stripes bright against the dusty ground. Hordes of parents and baby-sitters pushed strollers around, and kids ran everywhere.

"My dad used to take me to the zoo in Detroit," Avery told him at the end, as they started for home. "I was really little then. I used to like the elephants best. Did you know elephants will baby-sit for each other's baby elephants?"

"No, I didn't know that," said Jere solemnly. He felt apologetic. "They don't have elephants here. But they're going to get some lions next year."

They went back a couple more times during the summer, but they hadn't gone yet this fall.

His father dropped Jere and his mother off and went on to work. By the time Jere had showered and changed and had something to eat, he was feeling better. He had to do a couple of chores that he could tell were invented rather than necessary: Carry some trash cans up from the basement and put them in the back of the garage. Walk to the hardware store for lightbulbs. Sweep the sidewalk in front of the house. There must have been all of eleven leaves out there. His parents fussed about the outside of the house because the park was right across the street, and they thought people would notice if the house looked messy or shabby.

When he was off the hook, he called Avery. "Can you leave pretty soon?" he asked.

"I think so. My mom's been after me all morning."

"I'll start riding over now."

Avery and her mother lived in a new condominium building a fifteen-minute bike ride away. Jere propped his bike up in their front hallway.

"Why don't you bring that in here while you're gone?" Avery's mother suggested. She was younger than Jere's mother, and she had pretty blue eyes and soft blond hair that curled all around her face in a pleasant sort of confusion. She didn't seem at all flaky. She taught English at an adult education center. She and Avery's father were divorced. From the photos around the room, Jere knew that Avery had some of her father's looks, but there was something about her that looked like her mother, too. Maybe they had the same expressions, the same gestures—it was hard to put your finger on it.

Avery came out wearing skintight blue jeans, a short white shirt that left several inches of tanned waist showing, and olive green sneakers with huge platform soles. Gold hoops flashed in her ears, and she had on a lot of black-red lipstick. "Hi," she said to Jere. She picked up a miniature backpack that looked like it was made out of a rug and slung it over her shoulder. "See you later, Mum."

They walked to the bus stop at the end of the block. Avery pulled out a pack of cigarettes and lit one while they waited. She looked just like all the other tough girls standing on street corners and outside convenience stores. Some of them were a lot younger than she was. She got only a couple of puffs in before the bus hissed up. She threw the cigarette down and tramped it out.

The bus rocked and bounced through a burned-out abandoned neighborhood, then along streets that were shabby and trash-strewn, but lively with people—women carrying shopping bags, men leaning together beneath the open hood of a car. It took about twenty minutes to get there. Avery swung off the bus first, and Jere jumped off after her.

The entrance to the zoo was marked by a huge stone arch commemorating some long-ago event that had to do with a war, not one of the wars Jere had heard of. The ticket booth enclosed a cranky senior citizen wearing a turquoise shirt embroidered with the zoo logo. He took their money, handed them their tickets, and looked impatiently at his watch, as if pretty soon he was going to pick his booth up and move it somewhere else.

Jere stuck his change in his pocket, and they were in. He loved this moment, when they first started up the long grass pavilion that ran the length of the zoo. There was nobody they knew anywhere in sight. It was like being in a new country.

They liked to begin at the African Rain Forest House, way at the other end of the zoo. As they pushed through the first set of metal doors into the entrance hall, a bird screeched somewhere. The second set of doors opened into hot, damp air, birdcalls, the sound of rushing water. High above them, glass ceiling panels, opaque white, suggested a limitless sky. A bird with long orange legs stood on a high rock, tucked in its black wings, and let out a startling scream. It lifted itself into the air, its legs dangling down like afterthoughts.

Right in front of them, across a moat barrier, a huge gorilla lounged on a rock. He picked up a stalk of celery, looked at it, took a bite. He moved around the rocky hill on feet and knuckles, settled on his behind, chewed some more. His fur was luxuriously thick. He raised his eyebrows, smacked his lips over the celery, and scratched his backside with long, leisurely fingers.

As he was watching the gorilla, Jere became aware that a man was standing nearby in a shadowy corner. He was short and stocky; his head was up as he watched the tops of the trees, watched the birds. The man seemed to notice Jere's attention, glanced at him over his shoulder. Something about the way he looked at Jere—the way his head turned, or the set of his dark, wide eyebrows—gave Jere a peculiar feeling in the pit of his stomach.

Jere might have known him from somewhere, a long time ago.

"Let's go check out the hippos," said Avery.

A few yards away and around a corner, a pair of pygmy hippopotamuses floated in a swampy enclosure. Little tufts of ratty hair grew on their ears, and every few seconds they would twirl their ears, sometimes both at once, like eggbeaters, sometimes one and then the other.

A little girl wearing a yellow playsuit, yellow socks, and yellow hair ribbons darted up and pointed at the water. "Ew! There's something in there!"

A boy shoved past her and threw himself at the guardrail. "Lookit, it's going under!"

One of the hippos slipped silently beneath the water, a bulky shadow moving away.

"Now you've scared it," Avery said to the girl. "It hates yellow." The girl's father gave Avery a look and pulled his daughter away. Avery sometimes said these things that were a little off-the-wall, and Jere would have grinned, but something was making him tight and uneasy.

Avery moved on around the corner and stopped by the python's glassed-in cubicle. "Isn't it weird when you can't see the snake at first, and you look around, and you think it isn't there, and all of a sudden you realize it's curled up about three inches in front of your nose, and you thought it was a branch or something." They peered in all the corners of the cubicle and saw nothing. "Must be out to lunch," she said.

They walked farther and came to an area with two saddle-billed storks on one side and a pair of warthogs on the other. "Talk about lunch," Jere said. He nudged Avery. A brown mouse dangled by its tail from the tip of one stork's bill. The stork dropped it, picked it up by the head, swung it around, and gulped it down.

"Oh, ugh! *Yuck!*" Avery made a face and flailed her hand in the air.

"How do you like your mouse?" said Jere. "On a whole-wheat roll or plain white?" Now he felt better.

Avery gave him a shove and turned into the zoo shop. They picked through a stack of T-shirts with new designs, tried out a running-water bamboo whistle four feet long. Avery stuck it back in its bin. "How about the birds?" she said.

As they pushed through the exit doors, Avery's hand knocked against Jere's. He thought she might be going to hold his hand—she had done that once or twice before—so he kept his fingers limp and still, not grabbing at her, but available just in case.

Not this time.

The free-flight cage was an open-air cage that soared four stories high and covered about an acre of ground. An elevated walkway zigzagged through the exhibit. To get in you had to go through what felt like a small jail cell: There was an outer door, which closed behind you, and then an inner door. It kept the birds from escaping.

Avery pushed through the entrance first. Jere felt a quiver of nervousness as he followed her; he didn't like the feeling of being shut in, even though he knew the doors weren't locked.

A family was leaning on the rails by the entrance. The father was reading a sign in a droning voice: "'The main diet of the crested roving tweak...'" Farther along the walkway, two mothers were pushing strollers with squirming toddlers belted in.

"God love us, will you look at that?" One of them stopped and pushed her stroller back and forth. "Look, Joshie, look—see the bird? See his feathers? Green feathers, Josh. Can you say *green*?"

Josh screamed, "No green!"

"See the green bird, Julie?" chirped the other mother.

"Green bird!" Julie crowed, watching her mother.

"Good girl!" squealed her mother.

"Sharon, she's so *smart*," said the other mother. "Isn't Julie smart, Josh?"

Josh threw a handful of animal crackers onto the walk and stiffened his legs and screamed, "No green!"

"You know, I think it's time to get out of our stroller for a while," said Josh's mother. She cracked her gum. "Say bye-bye to the birdies, Josh. How about we get a drink and sit on the grass?"

The entrance doors to the flight cage closed with a *clang*, and the screaming faded. There was a sudden hush. Jere and Avery moved as quietly as cats along the bends of the walkway. Jere couldn't see more than a few yards ahead, and the trees growing up past them made it seem as if they were floating in a woods, in a place magically set off the ground. In the pond below, two ducks bobbed, poking their bills into the gurgling water. Avery looked over at Jere and giggled.

They went around another bend, and Jere saw a man in a windbreaker standing near some ducks on the bank of the pond, in a place of dappled shade. The man was facing away and standing perfectly still, like an animal in camouflage. He threw a handful of something out to the ducks, and they waddled toward him and began picking it up with their bills.

"Hey—you're not supposed to feed the animals!" Avery called out. "See the sign? It says don't feed the birds!"

You could never tell with Avery. One minute she was smoking cigarettes; the next, she came on like a little police officer.

The man turned around and looked up at them. He was the one Jere had seen before. Under his jacket he was wearing a turquoise shirt—one of the zoo staff. A strange feeling crept up the back of Jere's legs.

"Oops—sorry!" Avery shrugged. "Sorree!"

The man continued to stare up at them.

"Let's get out of here," Avery said under her breath. "He looks mad."

"Wait a sec." Jere's heart was thumping. The man was looking straight at him. He had a wide white face with a square jaw and these very dark, broad eyebrows. His face was moving all around; the expression kept changing, as if he were listening to some internal dialogue.

Jere had a sort of sliding sensation, and for a moment he wasn't sure where he was. He knew this man. He had seen him before, just like this—the man looking up, Jere looking down.

"Are you okay?" Avery squeezed his wrist. She

began crowding him back toward the entrance. She smiled back at the man, some throwaway gesture of politeness. But she shouldn't have. Jere knew she shouldn't have acknowledged the man at all. She should never have said one single word to him.

They hurried back along the walk toward the exit, and as they pushed through the doors, Jere looked behind him. The man was out of sight.

"Was he weird or what," said Avery.

Jere didn't say anything. He clenched and unclenched his fists a few times to try to get back to feeling normal.

"Are you going to puke? Seriously." Avery stopped and touched his arm with tender concern, or as close as she could come to it. Sometimes Avery would be motherly like this. It was almost a joke. She was so skinny—undersized, really—and quick and unlingering, never stopping long enough even to pat a puppy; then she would be delicately solicitous, for a fraction of a second.

"That guy back there. I've seen him before. I know him from somewhere," Jere said.

"And so?"

"He's—there's something about him. I don't know where it was I saw him."

"Maybe in some other life," said Avery lightly. "My

aunt Diane says she's had out-of-body experiences. She gets premonitions all the time."

"Oh, great. Is this your crazy aunt?"

"She's only crazy about some things; she's smart about others. You ought to ask her about it."

Jere's head throbbed as they walked along the pavilion to the other end of the zoo.

"Well, I guess we're done for today," said Avery, giving him a glance.

Jere nodded.

As they waited at the bus stop, the sound of honking horns, trucks grinding their gears, and pieces of people's conversations around them made everything seem almost normal again.

"Maybe I made a mistake," Jere said.

"That was no mistake," said Avery, looking at him closely. "You turned green, Jere. Face it."

Chapter **TWO**

You turned green, Jere. Face it. All the way home on his bike, he kept telling himself it wasn't anything. He couldn't remember seeing this guy before today, at the zoo or anywhere else. Unless he had noticed him out of the corner of his eye one of the other times they went to the zoo—sort of seen him without seeing him. But that wouldn't explain the dread that had rippled through him when he first saw the man's face.

"Avery called a minute ago, believe it or not," his mother said when he walked in the door. "I thought you had just spent all afternoon with her. Are you seeing her tonight, too?"

"Don't know," he said. He called Avery back.

"James Wall's parents are letting him have a party. Want to come? Bring stuff, soda or chips. Starts at seven-thirty and goes to whenever."

"Sure. Okay. See you later." Ever since they had started being friends last year, Avery had made sure Jere got asked to all the parties she was going to. Sometimes Jere was still amazed that she was willing to be friends with him. She was the one who had picked him out, not the other way around. She'd come over to his locker one day in eighth grade and asked if he wanted to go home with her on the bus and do homework. She'd asked him, Jeremiah Straitlaced, Jeremiah Poker Face, Jeremiah Neat Clothes. Maybe he had some hidden magnetism after all.

He'd said, "Okay, sure," nodding and feeling his face turn red. Some xeroxed stuff slid out of his notebook, and he was sure he could smell his socks. While he was standing there nodding, suspended in his private bubble of shock and joy, it crossed his mind that she'd said something else. Maybe he'd heard her wrong—he had read somewhere about how you can want to hear something so badly that you do hear it, even though it isn't real.

"Okay, then, great! See you here after Mrs. Maybury gets through with torture!" Avery had given him one of those quick, flashing turns of her head as she walked away. Avery was *quick*—that was the whole thing with Avery. Jere had just stood there stiff as a wooden bowling pin, duh.

Eben Wax and Tim Mulhoney had immediately

shouldered up next to him. They had been watching from Tim's locker, three numbers away on the same side of the hall. "Heavy homework, huh?" Tim had said.

Maybe the party tonight would blot out the creepy feeling that still clung to him.

On Saturdays they all ate together, and tonight his mother had cooked something Chinese, or imitation Chinese, that he liked, even with broccoli in it. His father sat down at the table with an air of cheerful satisfaction.

"Finally finished that thing," he said. "Eighty pages. Now it's Marlene's baby."

"Good news," said his mother.

Not for Marlene, thought Jere. Marlene was his dad's secretary. His father was hoping to be made a partner in his law firm in the spring, and he had to put in all kinds of extra hours. He hadn't gone to law school till he was in his thirties, and now he was making up for his late start.

"James is having a party," Jere said.

"Would you like a ride?" his father asked.

"Well, yeah, I would."

"No problem. Your mother and I are going out to a concert. We'll drop you on the way."

"Thanks." It was always a good sign when his father

cheered up. He got pretty tense working the extra hours, and he wasn't exactly laid-back to begin with.

The party was predictable, and so it was comfortable. Mostly kids from his class, freshmen at Southern High. Avery's older friends stayed for a little while, then went on to some higher-ranking party. James had good tapes and CDs. There was plenty to eat—Doritos and corn chips and pizza. On the way over, Jere's father had stopped at a 7-Eleven, given him twenty dollars, and told him to get four six-packs, not just one. Jere had arrived with Pepsi and orange and ginger ale. He put it all in a trash can full of ice and other cans of soda.

Mr. and Mrs. Wall were there. There with a capital *T.* But later on, they would probably tactfully go upstairs for a while. Nobody in this group smoked dope or even cigarettes—not yet, anyway, and for sure not with parents right in the room. Nobody drank beer at the Walls'. The most that would happen would be in James's basement—two or three couples would fade away to a shadowy corner, sink onto the floor behind the couch, and grope around for a while. Kids who had more advanced things in mind would leave early.

The music was so loud it was actually kind of restful. Avery drifted by once or twice. She was with Kyle

Lamar, a tall, skinny guy who was two years older than she was and always cracking jokes. He'd shaved a little path around his head. He had his hand on Avery's waist, but Jere saw her wriggle deftly away. She hadn't come to the party with Kyle; he was pretty sure of that.

He mostly stood around. Every party needed a background lining of people, a ready audience for anybody who had to show off, and meanwhile they kept consuming food, so it looked as if they were doing something.

He was enjoying this sensation of being removed without it really showing when out of the blue the man's face came into his head again. The noise had created a space, and that was what stepped into it.

What was going on, anyhow? He started to reach for a handful of chips, but his stomach had turned to stone.

He'd been trying to brush the man aside, mentally speaking, but the guy wouldn't leave him alone. Okay, then. He would try to think of exactly where he had seen him, why his face gave him the creeps. Worse than the creeps, actually. He flipped through his memory files of nasties—traumatic camp counselors, mean lifeguards, scary characters in movies he shouldn't have been taken to. He had an older cousin he used to visit in the summers, and Harry was always hauling him off to do things they weren't supposed to do. Harry had taught him some valuable things about life, such as how easy it was to find your stuff if you left it out on the floor instead of hiding it in drawers.

Just thinking about Harry made him feel better. Maybe he'd give him a call, tell him he'd seen the bogeyman. Harry was in college now. According to the phone calls Jere's mother got from Aunt Maggie, Harry had not lost his talent for getting into trouble. If anything, it had broadened and matured. He said Jere should come stay with him in his dorm sometime provided he didn't get kicked out of his dorm—but not till Jere was older. Definitely had to be at least sixteen.

Jere crunched a handful of chips, felt like himself again. He followed Avery at a distance, with several people between them, to the other end of the crowded room. A few kids were dancing near the stereo. Now Avery was dancing with Kyle. Jere watched for a minute, nearly tapped Sandy Oates on the shoulder. She was watching the dancing, too, gyrating around a little on her own. She used to go to Sunday school with him; she always said yes. But he didn't. Instead, he found Eben, and they went over the soccer game.

*   *   *   *   *

When he got home that night, he undressed slowly, took a long time in the bathroom. He had had a pretty decent time, and he'd seen Avery go home with Crystal in Crystal's mother's car. When he finally got into bed, he reached over to turn out the light beside his bed, but then he let his hand drop, let the light stay on. It was ridiculous, but he was afraid to fall asleep. It was as bad as when he was a little kid. He lay on his back with his arm over his face, but he couldn't get comfortable. He turned over, punched his pillow up at one end, tried to settle in. What was he scared of?

He turned off his lamp. Then he lay still and looked up into the dark, holding his breath, feeling that he was about to step off a cliff.

He was trying to wake up. *You're waking up, you're waking up, you're waking up....* He had taught himself that trick when he was seven or eight and used to have a lot of bad dreams. By forcing the words into his dream, he could get the terrifying plunge from the tree or the wolf snarling under the bathroom door to fade. He would pass through a funny curtain of numbness, and then— snap—he was out of the dream, in his bed, in the world again. *You're waking up....*

He gasped, felt his whole body lurch, and wrenched

himself awake. He looked up at the ceiling, heart pounding. Where had he just been? It was going fast. All that was left was the last moment, when it was nearly dark, and a man was standing over something—a person on the ground. The man had made her fall down, but it was much worse than falling down—Jere knew it was. Something was terrible; she didn't get up. It wasn't a joke, it wasn't playing. The dream vanished as quickly as a cat slipping through a door.

Sick fear clung to him even though he had woken up.

He closed his eyes and instantly slipped back into the dream. It was getting dark, and the man had done something with his toy gun to make the girl fall down, and Jere shouldn't have seen it, but Jere was still looking at the dark street. He couldn't help it—he couldn't get his eyes not to see what he had seen. Now the man was going to turn around—

Jere gave a muffled shout and woke up again. He sat all the way up, rubbing his head. If this kept up, he'd have his parents shuffling in here in their slippers, wanting to give him back rubs and hot milk. He turned on his light. Four-thirty. Okay, he'd stay awake, then. No way he was going to have that dream again. He pulled out a paperback from his bookshelf and crawled back under the covers. The whole room felt alien with the light on; even his scattered sneakers and socks hated the bright light. He made himself read a few sentences. He nodded off, then jerked awake.

By the time the sun finally came up at six-thirty, he was exhausted, but he knew he was past having the dream repeat itself. He fell back asleep and didn't get out of bed till nearly noon.

He woke to a silent house. He pulled a sweatshirt on over his pajamas and padded downstairs in his bare feet. His parents were nowhere in sight. They must have gone to church. Jere helped himself to a bagel, picked the sports section out of the Sunday paper, and went outside to the patio. It was freezing. He sat there for a while, letting his thoughts touch gingerly on the night before. Out here in plain daylight, the nightmare ought to shrink down to a bad night, a bad dream, over and done with.

He shook out the paper, folded it back to a story about the baseball play-offs.

He sent out a tentacle of memory toward his dream—testing, testing—and was relieved to find that the details were far away. The scene sat there like a stiff little cartoon. But it was like holding his breath. He had a feeling that the dream was waiting to get him. It was swelling out of a mental closet, getting ready to run right over him if he let it.

Now he didn't feel comfortable sitting on the patio alone.

He stood up, patted the sports section together, went back into the house, paced around the living room a couple of times, went back to the kitchen, poured himself some orange juice. He'd never had trouble like this with a dream before.

Maybe he should have gotten up and gone to church with his parents. The sound of Mrs. Ford's quavering soprano singing the offertory hymn would certainly have gone far in driving out one nightmare and replacing it with another. He dimly remembered his mother looking into his room and trying to get him up, but it was all he could do to raise his head an inch off the pillow, say no, and dive back under to blank, blissful sleep.

He didn't want to sit around, giving this bad leftover feeling a chance to seep into everything. If he started his homework now, he could get it done in maybe an hour, and then he could get Eben and Tim to go shoot baskets at school. The school didn't care if you hung around outside on weekends so long as you were doing something legitimate. Then maybe Eben and Tim could come over and watch TV—plenty of sports were on on Sunday afternoons.

He heard his parents drive up as he climbed the stairs. He hated admitting it, but he felt better when he heard them come into the house.

They shot baskets and watched a football game, and both Eben and Tim stayed for supper—spaghetti and garlic bread that was really loaded with garlic. There was no way he was going to tell his friends about the nightmare. It seemed as though the longer he didn't say anything, the further away it went.

He was uneasy going to bed that night, wondering if it was going to come back. He kept waking up all night long, but not because of bad dreams. He just couldn't seem to fall solidly asleep. By the time he had to get up for school in the morning, he was more tired than when he'd gone to bed.

Algebra was his first class, and he sat through it numb as an eraser. Math was one of his strongest subjects, but fortunately Mr. Best didn't call on him this morning.

He saw Avery at her locker between classes. By the time he had put his stuff into his own locker, she'd gone on her way to second period. Too late. Now that he couldn't, he suddenly wanted to tell her about his dream.

He had to make it through his classes, eat lunch, then go to soccer practice at 3:30. When he got home, he was too tired to worry about anything. After he'd had supper and finished his homework, he fell into bed and slept without waking once all night. Maybe that was all it was—getting too tired. Maybe the dream was gone now.

He deliberately steered away from thinking about it for the next couple of days. Once in a while, he wished he could mention it to somebody at practice, just to make himself feel more normal. But he couldn't think of how to bring it up. "Hey, had any good nightmares lately?"

He ran laps, did all the drills as hard as he could, forced himself to get totally tired physically. It felt good to have nothing on his mind but the endless commands of Coach Barker, who was always finding slackers.

After practice on Thursday, he took his shower and got out of the locker room as fast as possible. It was near twilight as he left the school. As he went along the sidewalk, he started to feel uncomfortable. The sports drills were over, the needle blast of the shower done. In the stillness, an edge of his dream suddenly brushed up against him like a dark wing.

Here we go again, he thought.

As he came in the door, he felt too tired to do anything. He had never realized how much concentration it took to keep yourself from thinking about something. You couldn't just give your mind an order and have it do what you said.

He didn't talk much at suppertime. They had pasta, which didn't take long to fix; they had it a lot during the week, different shapes on different days. His mother said he should start his homework, that she'd take care of the dishes later, because now she had some work to finish up. He could see a bunch of open law books stacked on top of one another on her desk in the study and heaps of papers slanting everywhere on the file cabinets. He dragged himself upstairs.

He sat down and stared at the unfamiliar sight of his own desktop, cleared of debris and dusted. Mrs. Everett came every other week to clean, and this must have been her day. He spread out his homework before him, but he could barely keep his eyes open. His pillow looked so comfortable; his bed, newly made up with clean sheets, was so inviting. He could have tried to keep himself awake, but he couldn't think why. He peeled off his clothes, letting them fall in heaps, and rolled into bed. It seemed that a part of him actually wanted the dream to start up again. He slid into the waiting darkness.

This time, the dream was telescoped—everything happened all at once. The man had already pressed the shiny thing against the girl's neck, and she was on the ground. The man turned, still holding his toy gun, and looked up, and Jere couldn't close his eyes or turn them away. The man's square, pale face was expressionless. His eyes glittered under heavy black eyebrows. In another moment, his stare would lift Jere right out of his room, through the window and down to the grass where he stood, and Jere would not be able to stop himself from seeing what the man saw, doing what the man did....

Someone was calling, "Jere, Jere," and then an enemy shone a huge spotlight into his eyes. "Jere? Jere! Wake up!" The light beside his bed was turned on. His mother was shaking him by the shoulder. "You're having a bad dream. I heard you shout from way down in my study."

"Wait a sec." He sat up, blinking.

"I thought I heard you talking in your sleep the

other night, too. Are you all right? Is something bothering you?"

"I've been having this nightmare. It'll go away. You didn't have to come in."

"You gave quite a holler."

"Sorry about that."

"Are you sure you're okay?"

"It's nothing, Mom, really." Why did he say that? If only he were eight years old again, he could ask her to sit on the edge of his bed and rub his back. But he wasn't.

His mother turned off his light. "Well, settle down and go back to sleep," she said, and she closed his door.

He wished she had interrogated him, insisted on knowing what was wrong. But in their family they never talked much about their feelings, especially not the queasy ones that came with bad dreams or getting nervous before games or feeling awful if you screwed up on an exam.

He could have told her plenty. He could have told her that he'd had a nightmare about a man shooting a girl, and the man knew Jere had seen him, and the man looked exactly like one of the bird keepers at the zoo. And Jere knew in his bones that he had had this dream before, a long time ago, when he was very young.

Chapter THREE

"**W**ell, you look like something the cat dragged in," Avery slung out cheerfully when she saw him the next morning.

"Thanks," he said.

"Going to play baseball at free period?"

He shook his head.

"What's the matter?" Avery asked.

"Just something weird. Nothing."

"They said I could catch. Walking home from school today? Want to go to the mall?"

"Okay."

She turned and ran off, her short black hair whirling like strands of silk around her ears.

Avery's friend Robin was sixteen and had a car. After school, Avery and Jere and a load of Robin's friends squeezed into the Toyota and rode to the mall.

Avery bought coffee and a muffin, and she and Jere

sat at a small, sticky table in the food court while she ate. Robin and the others—Chris and Leslie and John and Melissa—had gone off to the opposite end of the mall to the video store.

"Don't you want anything?" Avery asked.

Jere shook his head.

"Here—take half." She broke off part of the blueberry muffin, cradled it in a paper napkin, and handed it to him. He stuck it in his mouth, fluffy and sweet, the square crystals of sugar crunching against his teeth.

Avery was restless, twitching her foot. She wore black-and-gold-striped tights and slim black ankle boots that laced through shiny black hooks. She looked over her shoulder, took another sip of her coffee, nearly white with milk.

"So say something," she said. "Or else don't."

"Do you ever get bad dreams?"

"Sure, I don't know. Sometimes I get nightmares, don't you? I get tornado nightmares."

"Not a nightmare, but what about a dream that has a really bad feeling to it? And the feeling doesn't go away when you wake up?"

"Sounds horrible."

"I had this dream, and there was this man in it that looked like that guy at the zoo, the one in the bird place.

And he kills someone." He couldn't keep his voice steady.

Avery looked at him, her face suddenly narrow.

He felt all shaky. He curled the edge of his napkin between his fingers and watched them tremble against the tabletop. "It's really bugging me," he said defensively.

"My aunt says—" Avery stopped.

"Says what?"

"My aunt says sooner or later every dream comes true."

Jere groaned. "Not your aunt."

"She knows what she knows."

"Mind if we change the subject?"

"Fine."

"Fine."

"Fine!" Avery switched off her seriousness, popped the last morsel of muffin into her mouth. She crushed the paper debris into a neat little ball and stuffed it into her empty coffee cup. "Look, my aunt said sooner or later. Later can mean, like, *centuries*."

She took out a cigarette and lit it, then made a face. "Sometimes I don't even think I like these things."

"That's good, because here comes the security guard."

Avery crushed the burning cigarette under her foot and jumped up. "Time to go!" She waved her fingers at the guard.

They hung around the mall for another hour. Avery squirted herself with herbal perfume in a shop called Natural World and bought a bar of organic soap that smelled like Dial. She tried on a dozen pairs of shoes at Payless, then walked away without buying any, leaving them in a jumble on the floor.

"Aren't you going to put those back?" Jere asked. He followed her toward the exit. She sped up, and they scuttled past a clerk and between the metal shoplifting detectors and out into the central mall space. They wandered through the drugstore, into a toy store, past a vendor's cart selling baseball hats made to order.

"What did you say?" asked Avery.

"Did I say something?"

"You were mumbling." Avery shook her head and wrapped her arm around his waist and hugged him.

His game the next morning went by in a haze. The coach took him out in disgust after he passed the ball to the other team for the third time. By early afternoon, he knew he was going back to the zoo, though he wasn't sure what he was going to do when he got there.

He rang Avery's bell.

"She's not here," said Mrs. Cummings. "She went to the mall this morning with Crystal and Eva. Want to come in anyhow?"

What an idiot—he'd forgotten to call.

Mrs. Cummings's sofa was lumpy under the orange-and-gray Indian blanket. She brought him a can of cold soda; her fingers left dark prints on its dewy sides. She sat opposite him in a black butterfly chair that was worn to white threads on one corner.

"So," she said. "How's life in high school?"

"Just fine, ma'am," he said. He didn't know where that "ma'am" came from—he didn't usually talk that way.

"Any favorite courses?"

"Not really." He spread his hands, then took a big gulp of soda to cover up his lack of conversation. The soda was icy cold, and it made his eyes water. He could feel the fizzies gathering all in one spot partway down his throat, and then a ridiculous hiccup shot out. "Goodness, excuse me," he said.

"Canada Dry always does that to me," said Mrs. Cummings. "Oh, I forgot. Let me get you a napkin." She stood up and left the room.

He looked that bad, did he, that women automatically started reaching for napkins and drop cloths as soon as he came around? Yep, there went a trickle of ginger ale down the side of the can, crawling right on across the polished coffee table. Maybe he should have put it on the floor, but that seemed so manlike, so beer-can-like.

Here she was, putting a napkin under the can, not bothering to mop up what he had dribbled—probably didn't want to call attention to it, make him feel even more embarrassed. "I don't know why I can't remember these before I sit down," she apologized.

"Oh, that's fine. Oh, don't worry about it for a minute, please," he said, going overboard.

"Okay." She sat down again.

He drank some more ginger ale; it gurgled on its way down.

"Avery says you two are quite the zoogoers," she said. "I used to love the zoo when I was a girl. When Avery was little, her father used to take her to the zoo in Detroit. They had a train that took you all around, wherever you wanted to go."

"Oh, brother, that must have been great!" Why did he say these things in a superenthusiastic voice? Nerd. Dork. "You ever been to this one? It's got this African Rain Forest House, and there's a big outdoor birdcage, but the rest of it's kind of scruffy. Guess they need money."

"I'll bet they do," said Mrs. Cummings. "Maybe they'll have a capital campaign, or get some philanthropist interested. Zoos are wonderful places."

"Yep. You can go there and nobody waits for you to shoplift."

"No Big Brother watching you, hmm?"

"That's it. Plus—I like the animals. Animals are neat." Why did he keep saying these inane things? Where was Avery? "That's where I was thinking of going today, when Avery gets back. Did she say when she'd be home?"

"Around two-thirty, I think. She didn't say exactly. You're welcome to wait for her. I've got to excuse myself, though. I was doing some gardening out back. We've got some communal gardening space down there. There's a whole bunch of bulbs waiting to be put in."

"Oh, sure, that's fine. I mean, if it's okay, I will wait a little longer, just sitting here, unless you want some help. I mean, I could help you plant them."

"Oh, no, no, that's my recreation. I love to do it myself." She got up and collected her glass of iced tea and her keys and sunglasses, and Jere heard her go out the back door. He finished off the ginger ale, let himself give a long, satisfying belch. Then he got up and wandered around the living room, stopping to study the group of framed photographs sitting on the bookshelf. He'd looked at these pictures so many times while he was waiting for Avery. There were a couple of Avery as a little girl, one of a big group of people that had a cousins-and-aunts look to it, a couple of Avery and her parents. He always wondered about keeping photos of all three of them after the parents were divorced. It must be Avery that wanted that, and her mother went along with it. It wasn't the kind of thing he could ask about.

Finally, he heard footsteps and chattering female voices outside the door, and Avery came in with Crystal and Eva.

"Oh! What are you doing here?" Avery exclaimed when she saw him.

"That's okay." Jere began inching toward the door. He hadn't thought of them all walking in together.

"I must have forgotten. Did I forget you were coming?"

"No, no. I just came by, thought you might be here, and I talked to your mom for a while. It's nothing." Crystal and Eva were chewing gum and looking at him in dumb amazement from behind their carnival of self-decoration—shopping bags, mini shoulder bags, silver sneakers, tiny beads woven into little braids in parts of their hair and the rest in floppy ponytails and shingles of bangs sprayed yellow and pink. Something twinkled on the side of Eva's nose.

Mrs. Cummings came in, peeling off her gardening gloves.

Avery dropped her bundles. "So you want to stay longer?" she asked Jere.

"Nah—I got to be going."

"No, no, wait." She turned to her friends. "What are we doing?"

"We're meeting later on, remember? Laura's? Sleepover? Tonight?"

"Okay. So I'll come on my own."

"Okay, right. See you, Jere," said Eva in a heavy voice. Crystal walked out in step behind her.

"I'm going back to the zoo," Jere said. "Want to come? I can help you with your math when we get back." He added that for Mrs. Cummings.

"Now?" said Avery.

"Yeah. Why not?" Jere shrugged so hard, he felt like he was shrugging his whole body, not just his shoulders. He was not going to explain in front of Avery's mother.

"Okay, I'll come. Let me get some other shoes on." She brought out something that looked like a little girl's party shoes. They fastened with a single pearl button and were made of purple suede. She slung on her tiny backpack. "See you, Mom."

"You'll be back by five, won't you? For sure?"

"Promise!" Avery called over her shoulder.

"Why are we doing this?" she asked as they walked to the bus stop.

"I want to check that guy out."

"The guy who spooked you?" Avery raised her eyebrows and gave a tiny stage shrug. "Ooo-kay! What're you going to say to him?"

"I'm not going to *say* anything."

Chapter FOUR

The same cross old man pawed up their money through the hole in the ticket office window. Avery bought a diet orange soda, and they strolled up the pavilion.

"How do you know he's here? He might not work every Saturday," said Avery.

"Just look for anybody in a turquoise shirt," said Jere. They trailed maintenance men pushing garbage carts, walking with brooms. They circled sheds and buildings. Jere pointed to a man in a turquoise shirt scribbling on a clipboard by the reptile house. Small black mustache, dark golden skin. Not him.

Another man came out of the men's room—turquoise shirt, tall, bald head, cross-looking. Not him. An older man, small and wiry, with a sunburned nose, was emptying a trash can liner into a garbage cart. Not him. Two girls wearing volunteers' pins hurried past carrying aluminum pans of vegetables—carrot chunks, celery.

They tramped around the entire zoo twice and ended up by the entrance, near the refreshment stand.

"My feet hurt," said Avery.

"I can't help it."

"Ask somebody."

"What do I ask?"

"Can't you describe him?"

"Can I help you?" said a man standing near them. He wasn't wearing a turquoise shirt, but he acted like someone in charge. "Some exhibit you can't find?"

"There was a person we saw here last week—he works here, I think, and he...uh, he reminded me of somebody I used to know, so I wanted to see if that's who he was." Jere heard how lame he sounded.

"What'd he look like? I'm Ed O'Reilly, by the way. Assistant curator of birds."

"Jere Robison," said Jere with a self-conscious nod, "Southern High." What did he say that for? He couldn't believe himself. Looked like Avery couldn't believe it, either.

"So—this fellow you're looking for?" prompted O'Reilly.

"He's sort of medium height, brown hair," said Jere. "He was in the outdoor cage there, with the ducks."

"He was talking to himself," said Avery flatly.

Jere shot her a look.

"I bet I know who you mean," said O'Reilly. "You say he was talking to himself?"

"Mmm." Avery nodded.

"Has to be Al Watkins. That sound right? He's one of our bird people. He's probably in the free-flight cage, or else the Hanover Building. Tropical birds. I'll go over there with you, introduce you."

"No, that's okay, thanks." Jere began backing away. "We'll find him."

"Thanks!" said Avery in the special sparkly voice she used when she wanted to be extra likable.

"All right, then," said O'Reilly.

As they walked up the pavilion, Jere started to feel uneasy again. Maybe he didn't want to find the man after all. He sure didn't want to be introduced.

After the bright light outside, the Hanover Building was dark, and it took a minute for Jere's eyes to adjust. At first, the only other people he saw were a couple with their arms around each other, taking advantage of the low light and the solitude. He and Avery moved farther into the building. A musty, birdish smell clogged the air. It must have been built a long time ago, in the old-fashioned zoo style. A railing kept observers back from the glassed-in bird enclosures and their strange landscapes of artificial logs and branches. Some of the squares were empty.

A door opened at the end of the room, and a short, stocky, dark-haired man came out. He pulled the door shut, stopped to adjust something in the handful of buckets and tools he was carrying. A hot, sharp taste dried out Jere's mouth, and his stomach seized up. He nudged Avery. She laid her hand on his arm.

They turned and began to stare at the laminated toucan, which was hopping on twigs in the enclosure right in front of them.

The man hadn't noticed them. He began walking slowly across the middle of the room, in their direction. Jere turned outward a little bit to get a glimpse of the man's face. He could see that his lips were moving; the man shook his head, as if answering someone. He looked over at Jere but didn't appear to take any notice of him. He sighed, mumbled something, proceeded past Jere and Avery and out the door.

Avery slouched over in exaggerated relief.

"That was him," said Jere. He realized he had been hoping that the man would look different this time, that the eerie sense that Jere knew him would have vanished. It hadn't.

"So now what do you do? Ask him what he was doing in your dream?"

"Yeah, I just might do that."

They walked out of the building, back into the blinding bright outdoors.

"You see him anywhere?" asked Jere, looking around cautiously.

"Nope. Yoo-hoo, weirdo, where are you?"

"Hey, shut up!"

Avery giggled, looking a little uncertain. "He's gone—don't worry."

"You don't know that."

"Let's get something to drink."

As they walked back toward the zoo entrance, Jere kept thinking he saw short, stocky men in turquoise shirts. The man could turn up anywhere. Jere didn't want to encounter him in plain daylight. Something bad would come with him.

"Maybe we better just leave," he said. "What time does your mom want you home?"

"Five. We've got loads of time." Avery checked her watch. "I'm so thirsty. Come on."

They got in line at the refreshment window, then stood around and sucked their iced drinks down. Jere drank his too fast, and a cold headache shot into the top of his head. He pitched the rest of his drink into a trash can, and while Avery was slurping down the last drops of her frozen lemonade, O'Reilly came up to them.

"Say, that fellow Al you asked about?" he said. "Here he comes. I just paged him to help me with a couple of sick cranes."

The man walked right up; there was no way of avoiding him. He just stood there, too close to them. He didn't seem to know the right distance to keep. His face had a waxy sheen, and he had a funny smell, as if he had been eating popcorn.

"These two young people were looking for you," O'Reilly said to him. "Al Watkins, this is—?"

"Jere Robison," said Jere, suddenly scared and out of breath.

"You don't—" Avery tried to interrupt. "Avery," she said. She didn't give her last name.

Now O'Reilly looked at Jere. Jere couldn't get his voice down; it was coming out high, like a little kid's. "We—we saw you before, over there—I—I thought you were someone I used to know."

The man didn't say anything.

"Just someone." Jere shrugged. "But you're not." Now he was literally quaking. He knew he must look like a complete fool.

Watkins was still silent.

"Wrong...wrong identity. You know," Jere stammered. "You're not him."

The man nodded at them, moved his lips.

O'Reilly gave a short laugh, put his hand on Watkins's shoulder. "He likes to talk things over with himself!"

Watkins moved away from the hand.

"So, well, we're taking you away from your birds," said Avery, backing up a few steps.

"You can't do that," said the man, looking at her, speaking for the first time.

"No, no, I mean, we shouldn't, like, take up your time!" Avery stammered.

"I take care of birds," Watkins said.

"Right," said O'Reilly.

"You came before," said Watkins, looking straight at Avery. "I remember you."

"Right, well, sorry, bye," Jere said. He took a couple of steps back, expecting Watkins to turn away, the way people usually did when they parted company. Only he kept looking at them. "So long now," Jere practically croaked, and tried to grin; then he took off, feeling a crazy spotlight burning between his shoulders as he ran. Avery was right behind him.

Jere only wanted to get out of the man's sight, and Avery must have been thinking the same thing. Panic took hold. Instead of leaving the zoo—going to the exit, where they would have had to wait for the bus in plain sight—they raced side by side all the way back to the Rain Forest House. They ran around behind it and hiked up a path through a wooded section toward the old rose garden. No roses now; a big, chipped sign proclaimed that the garden would be restored in the future. They scrambled up a little hill and around some rocks and threw themselves onto a bench.

"God, is he a creep or what," Avery said. They both began laughing hysterically. "I take care of birds," she said, pitching her voice very low and going off into fits of laughter.

"I remember you. From before," said Jere. They both shrieked with laughter.

"Get away from my birds." Avery hung on Jere's arm and doubled over laughing.

In a moment, they calmed down. Avery fished in her

backpack, took out a pack of gum, and handed a stick to Jere.

"Look, this dream you were having—you know, with him killing someone? Dreams are only dreams. It doesn't have to mean anything."

"Oh yeah? Then why do I keep on having it?"

"You keep on having it?"

She crushed her gum wrapper thoughtfully, looked down, smoothed a circle in the dirt with one foot. "Can we go now? You don't want to see him again. Really you don't." She stood up and glanced around. He could be hiding behind one of the big old rocks, boulders the size of half-buried houses.

They walked the length of the zoo, checking behind themselves every few seconds. They went out through the stone arches to the bus stop. It was nearly closing time, and people were milling around the yellow T sign. The bus was already full when it pulled up. Jere crammed in behind Avery, and they pushed a few feet down the aisle. More people squeezed on through the rear door, and then the driver shouted something, slapped the door shut, and pulled away.

"You want to stay for a while at my house?" Avery asked as they lurched along.

"Sure."

They got off at Avery's stop. As the bus pulled away, Jere glanced back over his shoulder. In the window of the rear door was Al Watkins, squeezed up against the glass, looking all around, looking up and down at the buildings, as if he was trying to figure out where he was.

Chapter FIVE

"Why would he follow us?" Avery said. "I don't think he was. He probably lives somewhere out on the bus line."

"What's that?" Avery's mother had cut them slices of chocolate cake, even though it would ruin their appetites, and was sitting with them at the kitchen table. She pinched up some crumbs from the cake plate and popped them into her mouth. "If you don't mind my asking."

"Some weird man got on our bus at the zoo." Avery turned her cake around till the point was exactly in front of her and then cut a perfect triangle from it.

"He looked like someone," Jere said.

"Who?" asked Mrs. Cummings.

Jere took a huge bite of cake so he wouldn't have to answer right away, but Avery said, "Someone Jere had a nightmare about. A *murderer*."

"A what?" Mrs. Cummings stopped picking up crumbs.

"You tell her," said Avery.

Jere had to swallow three times to get the rich cake down his throat. "We saw this man at the zoo, and I had had this dream about him, that he killed somebody. It was just a bad dream, though." He didn't want to tell her the details, tell her how the dream had a grip on him, even though Mrs. Cummings was a pretty sympathetic type.

"You probably saw the man first and then had the bad dream," said Mrs. Cummings. "You've gone to the zoo several times in the past few months. That would make sense, wouldn't it? And you could get bad dreams just from reading the newspaper any day."

"I think I might've had it for a long time." That was all he was going to say. He didn't know what had made him say even that much.

"This guy looked like a wacko," said Avery.

"Well, whoever he is, keep your distance. It gives me the shivers to think he was on your bus. You didn't talk to him, did you?"

Avery gave Jere a look that translated, Don't say anything. She got up from the table. "I guess I've got to get my stuff together to go to Crystal's. Maybe I'll call you tomorrow about math. Okay?"

"Okay, sure."

Jere rode home slowly. He could call up a friend, try to get together tonight—it was Saturday, after all—but he didn't feel like it. He didn't feel like doing anything.

After supper, Jere and his mother and father all sat in a row on the sofa in the den watching television, some movie that was supposed to be a comedy. His mother had a stack of blue books to grade, midterm exams, but said she didn't want to start them till tomorrow; his father was waiting for a phone call and kept getting up and pacing around the hall until Jere's mother told him to sit down and relax. Jere couldn't believe it, really— here he sat, Jere Robison, with his parents, on Saturday night, watching TV. How bad could things get?

Even worse. He realized he wanted to tell them about his dream. He felt so stupid—only little kids did this. But he couldn't stand it. He got up from the couch and moved to a chair so he was facing them.

"Can we talk a minute?" he said.

"Well, sure," said his mother.

You won't sound so cheery when you hear this, Jere

thought. When he reached the part about the toy gun, his mother's eyes got huge. When he had finished, they both sat perfectly still, looking at him pretty much the way the man in the dream did.

"Gosh, what'd I say?" he asked, trying to laugh.

His mother turned off the television set and looked at Jere's father.

"What's going on?" Jere said.

"No one talks about it now," his mother began, "but ten years ago a young woman was murdered in Hiller Park, right across the street. She was attacked and shot by someone; they never found out who."

"Here?" repeated Jere. His pulse began to thud. "How come I never heard about it?"

"You probably did," said his mother. "You probably heard people talking about it when it happened. But it was so dreadful that after some time had gone by, people stopped mentioning it. I believe the girl's family moved away."

"Right across the street?"

"Yes. It was the day after Thanksgiving, late in the afternoon."

"Did you...see it?"

"We were downstairs in the study, but we didn't

know anything was going on. Your father and I were having a talk. And, well, later on we both felt guilty, because we didn't hear anything until the gunshot, and we didn't realize then what it was. A gun doesn't necessarily sound like a gun."

"We didn't feel guilty," Jere's father put in. "More like regretful."

"We didn't hear any struggle, any voices. If we had, it's *possible* we might have helped, though everything happened so fast, and because the girl died almost instantly, there's probably nothing we could have done. That's what the police said. Nothing anyone could have done."

"Who was it?" Jere asked.

"We didn't know her. A college student, they said in the papers, home for vacation."

"And it was right over there?" He looked toward the front of the house. He was starting to get scared of what he might find out. He felt as if someone had picked him up and put him down right beside the man in his dream, and from now on he wouldn't be able to get away.

His mother nodded. "Right at the edge of the park, by the curb. We'd put the storm windows on by then. They cut out a lot of noise."

"Where was I?"

"Up in your room, taking a nap."

"So I could have seen it from up there."

"I don't think so. When we heard the commotion outside, police cars coming and so on, and found out what had happened, I ran upstairs to get you. You were lying in your bed, on the other side of the room from the window, with the covers pulled up over your face. I thought at the time that that wasn't like you, but I decided it was one of those lucky coincidences. If you'd been over by the window on your rocking horse, you would have seen it all. I scooped you up and gave you a big hug. I guess I felt you had been in danger, too. When I picked you up, I could see over your shoulder out the window. I could see the police officers swarming around the park, and all those awful blue lights flashing. A crowd was gathering, and I didn't want you to turn around and look out and get scared. So I whisked you downstairs and gave you supper in the kitchen. You loved turkey and gravy, so I heated up some of that and made some rice, and you ate it all and didn't say a word."

Jere could almost remember that plateful of turkey and rice. He could imagine the two of them not saying anything much to him about this terrible event, having him eat supper and then acting as if nothing was happening, telling him it was best to forget about all the fuss, because they thought that would protect him.

"Did you ask me if I saw anything?"

"I remember I asked you if you had been taking a nap, and you said yes. And I probably told you that something bad had happened outside and that we were glad you were safe inside. I do remember worrying about whether you could have seen it and been too frightened to say, but you were so calm, so perfectly calm, it seemed unlikely. I probably should have asked you. I probably—"

"Susan, there's no need to go over and over what was done or not done ten years ago," said Jere's father.

"But he's just had a nightmare," said his mother. "What if he saw the murder after all? Children get traumatized by these things. We should have tried to pursue it then! We shouldn't have let it go so easily."

"He may well have *imagined* he saw it from what he overheard," said Jere's father. "Even if we were careful, all our neighbors were talking about it, and it was on the radio and TV."

"Do you remember seeing anything? Do you

remember seeing the murder?" His mother sounded frantic.

"I guess not," Jere said hesitantly.

"Look. Whoever he saw at the zoo, it couldn't be the same person who killed that girl," said Jere's father. "It goes against common sense. In real life, the man must have gone as far away as he could get, and he wouldn't come back. The police had almost nothing to go on, as I recall. Basically an unsolvable crime."

"Shouldn't he tell the police anyway?" asked his mother. "They might want to bring this man in for questioning."

"The police!" his father exclaimed. "Now wait a minute. So far, we're just talking about bad dreams here, aren't we? This is something that happened a long, long time ago. I'm not sure it's a good idea to go around digging all this up."

"It wouldn't hurt to tell the police," his mother said.

"How's it going to look if our names get into the papers, involved in some police business? This is the wrong moment for that."

"You mean with the law-firm types looking on?" said his mother. "We could keep our names out of the paper—Jere's a juvenile, after all."

"Let's give it some thought first," said his father. "You need a little more to go on before you call the police. And meanwhile, stay away from the zoo. Don't go looking for this fellow, for goodness' sake."

"So you think he could be the one?" Jere asked.

"I didn't say that."

He could hardly believe a murder had happened in Hiller Park and now was the first time his parents had talked to him about it. Could he have actually seen it? Maybe he had, and got so scared he jumped back into bed. But what his father said also made sense: that he could have formed a picture of it in his mind from what he overheard people saying. And he was young enough when the murder happened that he might have gotten mixed up about whether he really saw it or not. Still, his mother sounded majorly worried, and he hadn't made up Al Watkins from what someone else had said. He had found Al Watkins himself.

Jere couldn't very well call Avery at her sleepover. He waited till the next day.

"I never heard of a murder, but we didn't live here ten years ago," she said. "That's when we were still living with my dad in Detroit." She sucked in her breath. "Jere, what if it's really him?"

Jere swallowed. The telephone line carried a thick silence between them.

"He knows your name and everything," Avery said.

"Thanks for reminding me," said Jere.

"So did your parents make you call the police?"

"My dad said you have to have more to go on to bring in the police. My mom kind of wanted to, though."

"Mmm. Well, anyway, can I call you later and do math on the phone?" asked Avery. "I'm really tired. We were up all night. Guess what? Kyle crashed the sleep-over. Can you believe it? Crystal's mom made him leave. She drove him home at one A.M. He knocked on Crystal's window at midnight! Scared us half to death."

"Gee, that sounds great," said Jere in a voice like lead.

"But guess what? He came back! With Fish. And I snuck out with them for a little while. So Crystal's mother drove all three of us home the next time, around four-thirty. She wasn't too happy about it."

Jere didn't say anything for a minute. "Well, I'll be here if you want to call about math," he said finally.

"Bye."

*   *   *   *   *

She didn't call later about math or anything else. On Monday morning, every time Jere saw Avery, she was huddling with Crystal and Eva. They kept giggling and whispering, then pulling in other girls, who started giggling and whispering, too.

At lunchtime, though, Avery was waiting for him at the lunchroom door. They went through the cafeteria line together, then found an empty table at the back of the room. Avery waved across the room to Crystal and Eva, then sat down. "I told my mom about that murder," she said. "She freaked. That really did it, on top of the sleepover. She's so overprotective, I don't know." Avery sighed. "She says to tell the police. And if you don't, she will." She rearranged the pieces of lettuce on her plate.

"Maybe we ought to ask your aunt what she thinks, too!"

"Don't get sarcastic, Jere. My aunt is no dummy."

"I didn't say she was a dummy."

Avery located a ring of cucumber under her lettuce, speared it with her plastic fork, and dipped one edge in the little paper cup of salad dressing. "You know, my mom said maybe your parents aren't calling the police because they feel guilty."

"About what?"

"About, you know, how you could have seen the whole thing. I bet they feel guilty because you could be psychologically damaged."

"I'm not psychologically damaged! What are you talking about?"

"Oh, forget it. Anyhow, my mom usually does what she says she'll do. Do you want those crackers?"

Psychologically damaged. Just like Avery to come up with something like that. Probably read it in a magazine while she was getting her hair cut.

On Tuesday morning when Jere saw Avery in Spanish class, she didn't look so good.

"I saw him," she whispered as he brushed by her desk.

He slid into his seat. "Who?"

The teacher was passing out sheets of paper. What an idiot—a test, and he hadn't remembered. Avery picked hers up and looked ready to croak. He'd have to wait till the class was over to find out what had happened.

Señor Benzaquin rattled off something in Spanish that added up to "It is kindly time to sit down, shut up, and start the test." Avery began giving out little hisses of dismay and delicately biting the eraser on her pencil.

He figured he might get a fifty. One test didn't matter.

When the class was over, he and Avery left the classroom together, moving toward biology as slowly as slugs. "Last night, I went out to the parking lot beside our building—I thought I'd left some sneakers in the car—and I saw him walking up the sidewalk."

"*Who?*"

"The weird guy at the zoo, who else? You know he has that funny haircut? Kind of slanting down in back? And he was talking to himself."

He hadn't noticed the funny haircut. Naturally Avery would pick that out. "Did he see you?"

"I ducked down in the backseat of the car and shut off the light. I looked up a minute later, but he was gone. So I ran back in and went up to our apartment and looked out from my room—it's on the front—but I didn't see him anywhere."

"What'd your mom say?"

"I didn't tell her. She'd never let me out of the house again. I was going to call you, but I thought she'd hear me talking on the phone."

"You didn't call the police?"

Avery shook her head, looked faintly ashamed.

"Guess that means you're psychologically damaged!"

Avery gave him a shove and half a smile. "Don't say anything about how I saw him, okay? If he does come back, though, I'll really freak, I'm telling you."

"Me too." Jere gulped.

"What do you think he was doing out there?"

"Looking for the bus stop?"

"Jere! Unh!" Avery stamped on his foot.

The bell had rung, and they couldn't stand in the classroom doorway any longer. They put their notebooks on their desks and went over to the lab counters. Mrs. Springer began doling out worms. Avery's dissecting partner, Joel Hapgood, was staring at the tray. "Ohmigod, do we have to touch those things?"

"I'll do it—I like this part," said Avery smugly.

Jere looked down at the pale segmented length of preserved earthworm on his tray, then met the terrified eyes of Angela Garnet, his lab partner, and knew it was going to be up to him. He wasn't good at this the way Avery was—he couldn't get the cuts exactly the right depth, and somehow the stomachs didn't look like they were supposed to—but he did find all twelve of them, and it took his total concentration. It kept him from thinking about Al Watkins all period.

Avery got into the lunch line with Eva and Crystal, and Jere got in line behind Avery. When he had pushed his tray almost to the end and turned back to reach for a straw, he realized Kyle was right behind him. "How's it going?" Kyle said, and looked down at him from his six-foot height, bored to death. Jere picked up his tray and went over to the table where Tim and Eben were sitting. He saw Avery, Crystal, and Eva sit down at a table by themselves, and just when they had all their yogurt containers and plates of salad spread out, Kyle ambled over and sat down with them.

Jere looked away, as if he hadn't been watching and could have cared less. The guys at his table were rehashing a hockey game they'd seen on television. Nobody noticed that he didn't say anything, because he laughed in the right places. But he was starting to feel as if he were drifting far away. He could hear himself laughing when different people said things, but in his mind he was somewhere else, on an empty street in the half-dark, and down a ways was a murky figure, ambling slowly toward Jere, talking to himself.

Chapter SIX

He was definitely out of it at soccer practice that day. Too bad Kyle Lamar didn't play soccer. Jere could have planted a few kicks to the shins, rammed him with his shoulder accidentally as hard as he could.

After practice, Jere found himself walking toward the business district, the opposite direction from home. He'd never been to the police station before. The closest he'd come was the field trip his class took in kindergarten, and that was to the fire station. Well, he was going there now.

A nicely mowed lawn surrounded the low police building, and clusters of red geraniums grew under a sign: POLICE—DISTRICT 3. It looked more like a library than a police station. Jere pushed through the front door, wondering if they secretly videotaped everyone who came in, and went up to the glass-enclosed reception counter. Probably bullet-proof. There was a metal circle in the glass to talk into. Behind the glass he could see wall clocks, desks crowded into a small area, computers, and a door with one tiny barred window and a piece of paper posted underneath.

"Can I help you?" A police officer came up to the glass barrier, sounding impatient, looking tired: no time to waste on trivial matters. He had on a blue short-sleeved shirt, and his gun was conspicuous in its holster.

"I—I want to talk to someone about this man who might have killed someone."

"What was that?" The police officer leaned close to the metal circle, lost his tired look.

"N-not today, a long time ago, and now I've seen him again, I think."

"Stay right there. Let me get you in to see Officer Bradley," the man said. "Deals with juveniles. Hope she hasn't left yet. Just hold on." He raised one hand to keep Jere still and picked up the phone with the other. "Hi, Judy. Got a kid here to see you. You're not on your way out?"

The officer led Jere down a side corridor and through a locked door. They threaded around desks, passed a barred window (Jere saw that a piece of paper beneath the window listed instructions for the juvenile lockup, but he couldn't read what they were), and climbed up a flight of stairs. Everything smelled like the post office.

Officer Judy Bradley motioned for Jere to sit down. She was wearing a white short-sleeved police shirt, and she was tan and had blond hair pulled neatly back into a ponytail. She was probably as old as his mother.

"How can I help you?" she asked, crisply folding her hands on her desktop and looking him in the eye.

She listened to him with complete attention, scribbling things down on a yellow pad. He described his dream and both trips to the zoo and seeing the man on the bus. He had a feeling he should have told the officer that Avery saw the man on her street, but Avery would really be mad at him if it got back to her mother. Probably it didn't matter; what was important was that the police were onto him.

"Let me give Joe McElroy a call," Officer Bradley said when he was finished. "See what he can pull from the cold case files." She spoke cryptically into the phone, hung up, and turned back to Jere. Her questions were very direct; she didn't waste any time making nice talk. After he had gone over everything again, she asked, "What makes you sure he's the same man?"

"His eyebrows, his whole face, just this feeling I got, like almost a message."

"A message?"

"Just, like, instinct."

"Did you hear voices? That kind of message?" she asked in a careful, neutral voice.

"Oh, no, nothing like that."

"Good." She sat back and tapped a pencil on her wristwatch. "A dream isn't an eyewitness account, unfortunately. Do you have any direct memory of the event? If you or someone in your family was an eyewitness, we could act right away."

"Not really."

She frowned, and he suddenly felt he had sunk a few levels in her estimation. How could he not remember?

"When this man came up to you at the zoo, did he recognize you?"

"He didn't act like he did."

"Of course you probably look very different now from when you were four. You would have changed more than he has. If he did see you back then." An officer came in and handed her a file folder. "Joe, thanks." She flipped through the papers in it. "You didn't come in with your parents. Any special reason for that?" He shook his head. No point in telling her his father didn't want the police around because he thought it made him look bad. "What do they do? Would they be home now?"

"Probably not my dad," said Jere. "He's a lawyer.

My mom's usually home by now. She teaches at a law school."

"We have a record here of a homicide occurring ten years ago on November twenty-ninth in Hiller Park. Young woman found with fatal gunshot wound to the head. How'd you get over here?"

"Walked."

"I'm giving you a ride home."

"What's wrong? There's not some kind of trouble?" Jere's mother was taking a dish out of the microwave and she nearly dropped it as Jere led Officer Bradley into the kitchen. Something smelled delicious—meat loaf or onions, maybe both. It was strange, the heart-warming smell and at the same time the blade of fright, the officer in her uniform standing in the kitchen. "What is it? Don't keep me in suspense!" His mother looked around for a place to put down the dish, shoved aside a stack of magazines and mail, and set it on top of a dish towel on the counter.

"Do you have a few minutes, Professor Robison?"

"Certainly. Do you want to sit down?" Jere's mother sounded perfectly calm, but when she pulled out a kitchen chair, she knocked it over. She and Jere bent down at the same moment to pick it up.

"No, that's all right. I won't take much of your time tonight. Your son came into the station just now and told me he's seen a man who may have committed a homicide several years ago. Has he talked about this with you?"

"Just the other night, he told us about the dream he'd had and about seeing this fellow at the zoo. We didn't know what to make of it; we weren't sure whether to notify the police or not."

It was a relief to hear Judy Bradley asking questions and his mother answering. The police would do what had to be done. That was their job. They didn't have any second thoughts or worries about digging it all up.

"Can we go look at Jere's room?" Bradley asked. "Do you mind, Jere? I just want to get an idea of what you could have seen from your window."

"Okay with me," said Jere.

His mother led the way upstairs.

Bradley stepped over the pajamas and tape cassettes without even glancing down. "Is this how your room was arranged back then?" she asked. "Where was your bed?"

"Against this wall," said Jere's mother. "He had some toys over by the window."

Bradley stood at the window and looked out. "Got

to admit, he had a ringside seat." Her beeper went off.

Jere and his mother waited in the front hall while Bradley used the kitchen telephone. She came out a moment later, heading for the front door. "I've got to go back to the station. I'd like to talk to your husband, Professor Robison. When does he come home?"

"Not till very late, I'm afraid. I don't think there's anything he can tell you that I haven't."

"Sometimes a detail gets overlooked; everyone has their own recollection of an event." Bradley took out a business card with her photograph on it and handed it to Jere's mother. "Ask Mr. Robison to call me tomorrow morning first thing, will you?"

"All right." She looked down at the card. "This doesn't need to get into the newspapers, I hope."

"Not at this stage. That's the last thing we want."

Jere followed Officer Bradley to the door. "So are you going to arrest him?"

"We don't have enough to do that yet. I'm going to go to the zoo and ask him a few questions. That's my job, though. Don't you go back there. Don't put yourself in a situation that could be dangerous. We don't want him to notice you. And we don't want him to disappear, either. We don't want to scare him off."

"Right."

"So for now, see if you can remember anything from that time. Any little thing you can come up with will help us."

Jere watched her slide into her patrol car and drive away. As the red taillights disappeared, fear rushed back into his stomach like soda gushing from a liter bottle. Officer Bradley seemed to take away with her everything clear and forceful and purposeful.

"Your father is not going to want to answer police questions," his mother said, closing the front door. "It's a sensitive time for him at work."

"I know, I know, he said that before. But what about me? I probably saw someone murdered when I was four years old, and all you care about is whether Dad wants to talk about it?" He hadn't realized he was so angry, so upset. He thought he was doing something definite by going to the police, but now he felt like nothing more important than a forgetful kid.

"That isn't all I care about!" She sounded shocked and hurt. "I feel terrible to think we somehow allowed this to happen to you. There was just no sign that you had seen a thing. And I suppose we wanted to put it out of our own minds, as well. Parents don't always do the right thing, Jere, no matter how hard they try."

His mother served their dinner, and Jere ate

quickly. He brought his homework downstairs so he could watch TV while he studied, but he couldn't keep his mind on either homework or TV. He tried to imagine Bradley interrogating the bird man, and he couldn't picture the two of them talking. His thoughts kept drifting back to the flight cage, the way it had felt like a different universe inside the high enclosure. The bird man had been standing there, so impossibly quiet—how could any human being be so inconspicuous?

Chapter SEVEN

Later that night, long after he had gone to bed, Jere woke up when he heard the front door open and close. His mother must have waited up for his father; he heard her voice distantly in the kitchen. There was no answering voice—just a sharp slam of something, like a drawer; then, a short time later, soft footsteps came up the hall stairs, and he heard his mother go to bed.

Jere didn't see his father at all on Wednesday. Once in a while, he tried to test his memory, to stretch out the edges, think back to when he was four, but he could only come up with the stock things that he was always able to remember: the Christmas morning when he found the red tricycle; a time when he'd fallen on the sidewalk and scraped his knees and his mother had carried him home bawling; putting a worm on a hook when his uncle took him fishing. He couldn't find a way to anything else.

On Thursday, he kept himself awake until he heard his father come in the door. "You're up late," his father said, looking up as Jere came down the stairs.

"I was just wondering if you'd talked to the police officer yet."

"We had a chat today." His father picked up an envelope, shuffled the handful of mail his mother had left on the desk.

"What'd she say?"

"She said it's extremely difficult to solve these old cases, but they do follow every lead."

"Did she say if she'd gone to the zoo?"

"She didn't mention it."

"So you don't know if she talked to him."

"Nope." His father shook his head. "I hope you're not losing sleep over this, Jere."

Jere sort of shrugged, sort of shook his head in a muddled way. He wanted to say something about Avery seeing the man on her street. But it was impossible to bring it up when his father wanted to hear things another way. His father would probably argue that it meant nothing, and Jere would be unable to think of a logical rebuttal, a compelling reason to press for its seriousness. All he'd be able to say was that he felt afraid. And with his father, he couldn't let his fear and neediness show. His father didn't like to deal with anyone who was needy or uncertain. It didn't matter who it was—a homeless person begging on the street or his own son.

The next day, Tim and Eben asked Jere if he wanted to go with them to see the new movie *Trackers* that night. It was Friday, and nobody had any games scheduled. As Jere left school, he saw Avery climbing into Robin's car for their usual trip to the mall. He walked home, taking his time, not cutting through the park. When he saw the police car parked in front of his house, his heart started to race. At least the police were taking action.

Judy Bradley was sitting in the living room, on the edge of the sofa, not settled back into the cushions. His mother sat beside her, looking tense. Jere said hello, grabbed a soda from the refrigerator, flipped the top, and sat down on a chair at the opposite end of the room.

"I want to bring you up-to-date," Bradley said. "I went to the zoo and had a little talk with Al Watkins this morning. Asked him where he was ten years ago, was he familiar with Hiller Park. He didn't say much, didn't ask what it was about, just said the only place to reach him was the zoo. He did say he had lived here ten years ago. He's a strange one all right."

Jere nodded, realized he was holding his breath.

"I also talked to Everett Maynard, the director of the zoo, and this fellow Ed O'Reilly you mentioned, who's Watkins's supervisor. Watkins has been employed by the zoo for several years. Keeps to himself; nobody really knows him. He always shows up for work, is very good with animals. Especially with birds." Bradley gave her ponytail a flip to the side. "How are you good with birds? Beats me. Anyhow—he has an address but no phone. Just now, I drove by the address he gave. Looks like an abandoned building. I'll go check it out later. The zoo had a photo ID in its files, so we took that to copy it, run it through the computer, see if it brings up anything."

Bradley turned to Jere. "Any luck with those direct memories?"

"Sorry." Jere shook his head, feeling like a dunce.

"What about the idea of hypnosis?" Bradley looked at Jere's mother. "We've had good results with children, though of course it must be done with the parents' consent. And the child has to want to participate."

Jere's mother sat up straight. "We'd have to think very hard about that."

"Listen." Jere suddenly sat forward. If he was going to say anything, he had better say it now. "There's something else you should know about. My friend Avery, the one with me when we saw him on the bus? She saw him on her street."

"What!" exclaimed his mother.

"When was that?" asked Bradley.

"Monday night."

"Oh!" Bradley groaned. "Why didn't you tell us? Where does she live?"

"Montgomery Avenue—South Montgomery, over in East Point."

"We can send a car over there. I better go myself and talk to Avery—what's her last name?—and her mother. Can I get their phone number from you?"

Jere wrote out Avery's name and phone number on a scrap of paper.

"You'll hear from me," Bradley said as she started down the front steps.

His mother closed the door. He was in trouble now. "Eben and Tim asked me to go to the movies tonight," he said quickly. "I told them I'd go. Eben's dad is driving us."

"Now, just wait a minute. Maybe tonight's a night to stay in. I wish you had told me about this business— Avery seeing him on her street."

"I—she was afraid her mother would get too upset

if she found out. She'll find out now, that's for sure."

"They seem to have a few problems with communication," said Jere's mother. She frowned. "So do we, don't we?"

"So can I go to the movies?" he asked after a moment.

His mother sighed. "I can't lock you up. I don't like the idea of your going by yourself, though. Is Eben's father bringing you home? I don't want you out on your own at night with that man still around somewhere."

"We'll get a ride," said Jere. "I promise. If not, I'll call and you can come get me." He went upstairs to change his clothes.

The movie started. Ordinarily, Jere loved the moment when the lights went down, the screen was flooded with racing images, and the sound track filled his ears—he was caught. He liked the way the dark took him away from himself. But it didn't work this time. The movie started, and Jere's mind wandered. He couldn't seem to get into it. The sound was too loud, and the movie was boring. He was still aware of himself sitting in the darkened theater with Eben next to him eating popcorn and Tim on the other side of Eben, unwrapping a candy bar. The smell of the popcorn made him uneasy. He turned

around to look at the rows of faces behind him, all illu-
minated by the flickering screen. The woman directly
in back of him glared at him, as if he'd tried to look
down her dress.

He didn't see the bird man anywhere.

Eben's older brother came to pick them up, not his
father.

"You taking me first?" Jere asked. "Mind if we go
sort of out of the way?"

"No problem," said Seth. "Tell me where."

Jere directed him to Montgomery Avenue. As soon
as they turned onto Avery's block, Tim and Eben began
hooting. "Say, which window is hers?" they teased him.

"Too bad we don't have binoculars," Tim said.

"That's not what I'm doing," Jere said.

"Mm-hmm. Want us to drop you off?" said Eben.

"Yeah, right. Come back for me around eleven
tomorrow morning, okay?"

Jere craned his neck and looked up at Avery's windows, still lighted. He looked all along the sidewalk. He
couldn't see any people sitting in the parked cars that
lined both sides of the street.

"How many times you want to go by?" asked Seth in
a willing voice.

"Give him a couple more times. She up there?" said Eben.

Seth braked abruptly, pulled the car into a sharp U-turn, and headed back down Montgomery Avenue. Tim and Eben craned their necks to see into Avery's windows while Jere scanned the cars, the dark sidewalks, the doorways of closed shops. There was a French coffee shop still open; a couple of women sat at the table by the window. That was the only sign of human life on the street.

"Ah, forget it. Let's go," Jere said as they stopped for the red light at the end of the block.

"Anything you say." Seth peeled away from the intersection.

"Dad'd kill you for that," said Eben with a grin.

"How's he going to know?" said Seth.

They dropped Jere off a few minutes later.

"What'd I tell you? My mom had a fit after the police officer left. She went ballistic about why I didn't say something sooner. She says now I can't go anywhere by myself, though why would I want to anyhow? And she's going to drive me everywhere—here, school, everywhere. She barely lets me look out the window.

Someone might be standing on the sidewalk, looking up."

Avery sprawled sideways across her bed. It was Sunday afternoon, and she was supposed to be studying her math textbook, propped beside her on a pillow, but she kept falling backward and sticking one leg up in the air and turning her foot so she could check out her new sneakers from every angle. "Plus, she found the cigarettes. I hardly ever smoke and I didn't want to smoke anymore anyhow, but I don't think she believed me, because, well, there were the cigarettes in my drawer. So I'm grounded. It's a miracle she let you come over."

Mrs. Cummings had said Jere could come only to help Avery with algebra. At the end of the two hours, Mrs. Cummings was going to drive Jere home, no matter how much they'd gotten done.

Jere sat at Avery's desk fooling with his biology lab report while Avery was supposedly deciding which problems she couldn't do. So far, he'd filled in his name and the date. The rest was a beautiful blank.

Avery rolled to her feet, stepped over to the window, and pulled back the shade a crack. "It was so creepy that night I saw him. I was digging around in the car, and I happened to look up—I don't know why, something just told me to look up—and there he was, not that far away." She let go of the shade. "Do you think he saw me?"

"Well, if it was dark and all," said Jere, "how could he? Even if he did, how would he know it was you? He only saw you a couple of times. Why would he care?"

"He wouldn't." Avery chewed her lip. "Why do you think he was there?"

"I don't know. He's crazy."

"Oh, great." Avery threw herself back onto the bed. "God, I hate homework on Sunday afternoons. Doesn't it make you depressed?"

For all the next week, Jere did what Officer Bradley had told him to do. He stayed out of it. He didn't go back to the zoo. He went around doing all his usual activities, which boiled down to homework and soccer. He spent a lot of time alone.

Avery caught up with him one day in the lunch line. "Haven't seen *him* again," she said as she piled croutons on top of the lettuce on her plate. "Maybe they've got him by now." She looked expectantly at Jere.

"I think they'd tell us, because I'll have to go down there, too," said Jere.

"They're probably just not ready for you yet," she

said lightly. They both knew that wasn't true.

Jere noted with satisfaction that Kyle was nowhere in sight. If he was moving in on Avery, the job wasn't complete yet.

The next weekend went by, and still the Robisons didn't hear anything from Judy Bradley. Sometimes Jere pictured Bradley arresting Watkins. Then Jere would go in, and as he entered the police station, the memory of the whole event would come back to him, clear as a bell. He would tell what he remembered, and they'd lock the guy up for life, and it would all be over and done with. He wondered if the dead girl's parents would like to know. He hadn't thought much about the girl herself.

He decided to go to the police station again on Tuesday after practice. It was going on two weeks since Bradley had been at their house.

A police officer showed him to Bradley's office. She looked up from her desk with a smile and invited him to sit down. "The news is not so good, I'm afraid. Nobody has seen him for over a week. He hasn't been to work. Since they can't get in touch with him, they don't know if he's sick, but I doubt it. I think he got suspicious and flew the coop, so to speak."

"He's gone?"

"Looks that way. Who knows? When a guy has no connections with other people, it's hard to trace him. He probably has money to survive on, since he's been working. He could go to another part of the country, take a new identity, start over. One thing we can do is alert other zoos across the country and send out his photo—someone with his fixation on birds, there's a chance he's going to head for the same type of situation."

"How can he just disappear?"

"Doesn't seem fair, does it?"

"He's got to be someplace."

"There are all kinds of ways people can go into hiding. It's possible he's right in the city. People have been known to live in abandoned subway tunnels. But he has the resources to leave the area, and I suspect that's what he's done. I think just those few questions I asked him must have made him nervous. Now at least we do have a reason to arrest him. I asked him to be available, and he fled. We can mount a broader search for him now. I wish I had something more I could tell you."

Jere stood up and began to pull his jacket back on.

"I'm still trying to remember," he said.

"Good. And listen: Call me if you see him, even if you *think* you see him."

He said he'd be okay walking home.

It was nearly dark outside, and as he stood on the sidewalk, waiting to cross the street, he felt suddenly frightened. There was the safe haven behind him—the scruffy, overlighted police station with its ringing phones and wall clocks and police officers coming and going and trading jokes and insults with one another. Even Judy Bradley's blond ponytail looked cheery. Out here, he was nowhere; he was no one. He could see drivers frowning at traffic or talking on their car phones. They were warm in their cars, with the windows rolled up, something on the radio. Warm and safe. None of them saw him shivering on the curb, grit blowing around his ankles.

Maybe the police thought the bird man had disappeared, but what that meant to Jere was that he was no longer findable by logical searching. Jere had a feeling the man had been somehow released, that he was drifting around like a sooty shadow, that he could be anywhere. The range of possibilities now was infinite.

Chapter **EIGHT**

Jere's father declared that was the end of Al Watkins. His mother said she would be surprised if it was.

"I guess he's gone," Jere said to Avery the next day. A few weeks ago, he would have phoned her right away to tell her, even though it wasn't exactly a news flash. It wasn't like the bird man had disappeared at 7:32 A.M. on the fourth Monday in October. But he didn't call Avery any old time anymore. Her mother wouldn't let her talk on the phone while she was grounded. And he sometimes saw her with Kyle between classes.

Avery kept on gathering up her biology papers and slipping them neatly into her folder. She had a way of always arranging the little things in her life, patting them lovingly into place; it was the big things that tended to wander.

"Really?" she said finally. "That's funny. But—good." She bit her lip. "You want to come by and tell my mom? Maybe she'll let up on the grounding."

*   *   *   *   *

"How do they know?" asked Avery's mother.

"He didn't come to work, and the address they had for him turned out to be this abandoned house—no phone, either." Jere clasped his hands around his knees, unclasped them, leaned forward, twirled a little brass dish that sat on the coffee table. It skittered toward the edge, and he clamped his hand over it to stop it.

"I don't like this vanish-into-thin-air business," said Mrs. Cummings. "I'd like to know they've caught him. That officer did say they'd have a car out on our street twenty-four hours a day. And anyway, what could happen in broad daylight? But the murder—that happened during the day, didn't it?"

"Twilight," said Jere. "It was just getting dark, that in-between stage, you know, where it's still light but it's all blue." He stopped.

Avery looked at him. "Thought you couldn't remember anything."

"Me too. But just now—this is weird—I saw myself looking out the window, and the park was all blue, and it was that time of day that scares you when you're little, when you're afraid that things you don't want to have happen might suddenly happen."

"Do you think you're actually remembering?" Mrs.

Cummings asked quietly. "Sometimes the harder you try, the more you can't remember something, and then, when your mind's on something else, there it is."

"If I could remember, they could arrest him the minute they see him."

"If they ever see him again." Mrs. Cummings shook her head. "Our whole building is jumpy these days, especially the elderly people. They want to have a meeting about security; someone found a basement door unlocked one day. And then some people say that outsiders are using their parking spaces instead of the visitor spaces, and they want us to start giving out tickets. Can you imagine? Our own private tickets."

Judy Bradley seemed to be right. From every sign, the man was gone.

Another week went by. Avery told Jere she had gotten tired of looking out onto her street all the time. The more you didn't see something, the surer you got that you weren't going to see it, and pretty soon it was too much trouble to keep on being afraid.

One day Jere saw Kyle and Avery leave school together, and they were standing around at the bus stop when Jere walked past. Avery waved at him, and Kyle flapped his hand in Jere's direction and called out,

"How's it going?"—the only thing he ever said to Jere. Kyle was wearing a black baseball cap turned backward, possibly to cover up where the shaved place was growing in. The bus pulled up, and Jere didn't stay to watch, but he knew they got on together. So Avery must not be grounded any longer.

Seeing them together gave him a worse pang of regret than he wanted to admit. Being friends with Avery was the luckiest thing that had ever happened to him. But maybe she hadn't liked all that going to the zoo—maybe it was so uncool and she'd actually hated it. Maybe she didn't like getting into this thing with the weird guy. It was really Jere's fault, after all.

Jere couldn't get his mind off the bird man. Sometimes he tried to imagine where he himself would go if he had to hide out. He didn't think he could stand a subway tunnel. But there might be plenty of other out-of-the-way places. He had read about gangs of teenagers living in abandoned buildings, hooking up their own electricity, stealing food and blankets. He sort of liked the idea of doing it with a whole group. It seemed unendurable to go into hiding alone.

Sometimes he tried again to remember what he had seen when he was four. He could still recapture the surprise of that blue air, of something awful about to happen in the quiet park. The blue air was full of this thing that was about to happen, and he couldn't do anything but sit and watch, frozen behind the glass of his bedroom window. The memory stopped there.

The more he couldn't remember, the more frustrated he felt, the more he wanted to grab at it. He wasn't sure of all the reasons why. It would still count as eyewitness testimony, of course; that was important. But there was something else. He wanted to know how it had been for him back then. Whatever had happened was haunting him. He didn't want to stuff it out of sight, forget about it, the way his father wished he would. He wanted to be rid of the feeling that he was still involved, that he would never be free of what he had witnessed.

One day, he went to the public library. The librarian at the reference desk showed him where the microfilm machine was and assured him that their newspaper files went back much further than ten years.

He had remembered the exact date ever since Officer Bradley had read it out from the police files. He searched the metropolitan paper for November 29, the day after Thanksgiving. The story was on the front page. WOMAN MURDERED IN HILLER PARK, read the headline. It sent a shock through him to see the photograph of the familiar park right across from his house, the same stretch of trees and grass and curb that he looked out on every day. He read on.

The girl's name was Valerie Minton. She had been a senior in college, known among her classmates for her activism in environmental causes, especially those involving animals. She had a brother and a sister. There was a high school photo of her, one of those smoothed-out ones. Jere could see the spark of energy showing through the posed smile and the perfectly neat dark hair. This girl had not had the faintest idea of what was about to happen to her that Friday. Just walking home from the drugstore. The next thing, you're on the ground, dying. He wondered if she had seen him watching from his window. In his dream, the man always looked so intently at him. Had Valerie Minton also had a glimpse of him? Had she had a moment's hope that he would come to help her?

He wished he hadn't thought that.

He turned off the machine and left the library in a hurry.

Regular life went on. He finished the soccer season, glad to be done with the freezing-cold mud and the effort of making himself try harder. It was getting so he could hardly keep his mind on the game. His homework was starting to slip, too. He just couldn't concentrate for very long at a time. His mother put his laundered uniform into his bottom drawer to wait for spring. She cleaned his cleats and put them on the back shelf of his closet. He bought new basketball sneakers. Judy Bradley came by to report that she had nothing yet. Their search was continuing.

The weekend before Thanksgiving, Avery called him. That was something new. "Hey, long time," she said.

"I been busy," he said.

"Me too." She wasn't calling about math. Just felt like talking. The only interesting thing in her life was that their building was having a fit trying to figure out if some homeless person had gone through the trash one night after the bags had been set out. Her mother had to go to a meeting about it. She and her mother were going to go visit her aunt for Thanksgiving weekend.

It gave him a brief starburst of cheer that she had called. He was hoping she'd talk on and say something nasty about Kyle Lamar, but she didn't even mention him.

*   *   *   *   *

The Robisons planned to stay home for Thanks-giving—where else would they go? His father didn't have any family besides Jere and Jere's mother, and his mother's relatives lived on the West Coast. So there would be just the three of them and a small turkey, not one of those fat twenty-pounders they showed on TV. Jere's mother even threatened to buy a chicken.

Then, unexpectedly, his mother invited some neigh-bors, the Scotts, to come for Thanksgiving dinner. Mr. Scott taught physics at the high school, and Jere's mother had met Mrs. Scott at some library committee meeting. This had never happened before.

"What for?" his father asked.

"Just to have company, have a substitute extended family, you know. They have twin boys, younger than Jere—around nine, I think. Next year, maybe we'll go to their house."

"For Thanksgiving?"

"Well, yes. For Thanksgiving."

Thanksgiving morning was cold and sunny, just right for football. At a quarter to twelve, Jere and his father and Mr. Scott and the twins, Ned and Matt, walked over to the high school for the game. The white lines on the field, newly limed, shone in the sun. Jere sat with Tim and Eben in the bleachers during the first part of the game. He came back for the second half and sat with the twins and answered their questions. To them, he probably seemed nearly grown-up. Southern High won, which surprised everyone, even the coach.

It was midafternoon and the sun was already fading when they started walking home. The twins were acting out football plays as they went along, running and tumbling over each other and scrambling back to their feet. Jere's father and Mr. Scott were recalling the days they had sat on the bench during football games. Jere's jubilant mood over the win had left him quickly, and he lagged behind everyone on the sidewalk. He was starting to feel a little funny. The front yards they passed looked dead to him: raked and tidied up, the grass gone dormant, the shrubs and trees bare of leaves. The sun, low in the sky, gave off ominous reddish rays. The day before Thanksgiving break, he'd gone home with Avery, and Mrs. Cummings had given them cake, orange this time. She'd asked him what his family did on Thanksgiving, and she'd told him about this thing called the "anniversary effect," where you felt bad each year near the date when something sad or awful had happened to you in the past. You couldn't help feeling that way, because part of your self remembered the event, no matter what. Maybe that explained why he felt uneasy. Though he couldn't remember feeling this way on other Thanksgivings. Maybe he just hadn't noticed how he felt.

Jere's mother looked happy during dinner. When Jere was younger, she'd often had to stay at work until long past his bedtime, and on the nights when she managed to get home in time to tuck him in, she always used to say she wished she could work a little less and have a little more time for regular life. He would always say, "So just do it, then!" and she would say it wasn't quite as easy as that. Anyway, now she was doing it. The dining room looked so nice, the table set with linen napkins and silver knives and forks. His father was brusque but was trying to make polite conversation. The twins squirmed and left mounds of squash on their plates. Jere offered to take them to the park after dessert while the grown-ups had coffee and another piece of pie.

Jere helped the twins pull on their jackets, and they all stepped out into the cold. The boys took off ahead of Jere, racing across the street and toward the center of the park, where the climbing structure was. It was five o'clock, the long hour of dusk. Jere looked back at the house as he crossed the street. No face in the window this time. No cars were in the street; hardly anyone was out at all, except for one laughing family walking off their dinner. So quiet. This must have been almost exactly the spot where he had pulled out his gun and shot her.

The man was there first. He had been eating something from a little orange bag, and then he shook out the bag all over the ground, and the girl walked up and said something to him. Then he looked angry. She looked at him and stepped back—her hands in the pockets of her long, swinging coat—and then he said something and grabbed her arm, pulled her toward him, and put the barrel of the gun against her neck. There was no sound. She fell right down like a crumpling tower, and her long winter coat spread out over the ground.

Jere didn't want to remember any more than that; he didn't want to remember any dark pool spreading beneath her head, or the way one of her hands came up a little way into the air, as if to brush something away, and then fell limp by her side. Then the man glanced up, and he and Jere looked directly at each other.

Now the street was so still, the air so calm, the ground crisscrossed with dark shadows.

This was not the dream he was remembering. It was the real thing. Only now, instead of being a little boy inside the house, sitting still as a mouse on his rocking horse and looking out, he was standing where it had taken place. If he moved a yard farther to his left, by that rock, he'd be standing right where the man had stood. His feet moved, and he turned his back to the house and was looking down at something on the ground when the girl came up, with her hands in her pockets, and said something to him.

For a second, Jere lost hold of who he was; he felt a little dizzy. He stamped his foot. There was no girl coming up to him; he had no gun. He was not the bird man.

The twins were yelling. He looked up and spotted them halfway across the park, rolling around on the ground and pummeling each other. He went over to referee, but mentally he was barely there.

Now he had remembered. And there was no going backward, no forgetting again. Pretty soon he would go tell Judy Bradley. What could she do, though, but say they were continuing their search? He was on his own for now. He would have to follow what he knew until he came to its end.

Chapter NINE

The next morning, Jere went to the zoo by himself. A cluster of pigeons scavenged on the sidewalk just inside the stone arch. They made oily clucking noises, sounded like friendly little voices at first. But up close, pigeons were ugly, with their beady eyes and waddling bodies and sprawling orange toes. They ate anything. Disgusting. Jere took a couple of swift steps toward them, and they scattered.

He walked on slowly toward the Rain Forest House, looking at everything, not looking for anything. One pair of mothers stopped talking until he'd gone past them, and he wondered if he looked funny or something, if he looked like a loner, an oddball, someone people would avoid.

Jere gave a little chuckle when he thought of that, and he saw he'd startled yet another mother, this one with a baby in a backpack. She was tall, wore leggings and running shoes. She looked at him, then looked away. Maybe it meant nothing except that she had noticed him. It was hard to tell what was really in other people's minds. But, hey, he was right. She did think he was strange. When he swung around to walk backward, he saw the woman was still looking at him over her shoulder. He gave her a shrug—a sort of sheepish "I don't know why" look—and turned around just in time to keep from crashing into a cement trash receptacle.

His clothes would be different if he was a genuine weirdo. Grubbier. Probably would sleep in his clothes, never wash them, no showers, either. No toothbrush. Live on junk food, whatever he could find.

He continued toward the Rain Forest House. He wasn't sure what he was doing here, but it wasn't important to know. The zoo was a safe place. More animals than people, and animals aren't as fussy as people. You can move among animals and they don't care. Jere didn't want to think directly about the murder; his mind pulled up short and turned away from that. But he thought about the birds—the dirt of birds, their sounds, fluffy bits of feathers, their delicate feet.

He changed direction and headed for the free-flight cage. He pushed through the entrance.

He couldn't see anyone else in the cage. He moved along the walkway, stopped to look over the rail at the ducks waddling around the little pond. This was where they had encountered Al Watkins. Aluminum pans with rows of small silver fish sat on the opposite side of the water, where the ducks could feed anytime they wanted. They seemed so happy in their little swampy universe. They knew what they were doing—no wasted efforts, no plans gone awry. They were protected and safe; someone took care of them. A breeze brought the damp smells of pond muck to Jere's nose. Ducks liked that smell, liked the uncertain squish of mud around their feet, the taste of dead fish and weedy water. As they waddled around, their bodies bumped one another's like old companions. A small brown rat darted out toward the pans from the base of the fence, snatched up something in its teeth, scuttled away to eat it. None of the ducks paid any attention.

Jere walked farther along and stopped and leaned over the railing again. At this end of the pond, he saw a handful of orange crumbs strewn across the bank. Orange crumbs on the ground. Crushed-up Cheez Doodles, or whatever they were called. Not zoo food.

Jere felt as if he had been suddenly dragged up from deep water. Hadn't he remembered something like that—the orange bag the man was eating from? And then he turned it upside down and scattered something across the grass?

Jere was gripping the rail and staring so hard, he didn't hear the man come up behind him until a voice said, "Sorry, but we're closing the free-flight cage early today."

It was Ed O'Reilly. O'Reilly looked down at the place where Jere had been staring, shook his head. "We post signs, you know, try like heck to keep people from feeding the birds—but still it happens. A lot of junk food lately. At least that stuff down there won't hurt them. They love it, just like people do. They go right for it. And maybe the rats will get it first." He glanced at Jere. "I remember you from a few weeks ago, don't I? Weren't you the one looking for Al Watkins?"

"That's right," said Jere.

"Don't know what happened to Watkins. He just disappeared. Strange guy. Did you know the police were looking for him?"

"Oh yeah?" Now Jere was remembering the moment when O'Reilly had introduced Watkins, and Jere had smelled food around the man, like cheesy pop-corn.

"In connection with some crime, something serious.

You didn't know anything about that, did you?" O'Reilly looked at Jere carefully. Jere shook his head. "Well, he was good with birds. Handled them just right, you know, slow and easy, nothing to startle them. How'd you happen to know him? You specially interested in birds yourself?"

"Don't know anything about them. I didn't really know Al Watkins; he just looked like someone." Jere paused uncomfortably.

A rat shot across the open ground, nibbled at the orange crumbs, ran back to its hiding spot. "Eat your fill, my friend," O'Reilly said to the rat. Jere could tell O'Reilly was waiting for him to talk more, to show he had had nothing to do with Watkins.

"So what makes somebody choose birds?" Jere asked, trying to fill the gap. "I mean, if they're working at the zoo. Instead of gorillas or something?"

"Well, with most people it's some quality in the animal that they admire or feel at home with. They identify with the animal. Like take birds now. Birds can fly away, leave a situation just like that. Some people prefer birds of prey. Look at that Andean condor over there." He pointed to a separate section of the flight cage where a bird the size of a wheelbarrow walked across some stones. It stopped on top of one and spread unbelievably huge wings. "Ten-foot wingspan," said O'Reilly proudly. "She's people-oriented—that's why we keep her in a separate enclosure."

"Is she pretty tame, then?"

"Not exactly. I mean she goes after people when they're in her space. We usually take out the owls when the public comes through here, too. They're raptors, you know. Meat eaters." O'Reilly began moving toward the exit gate. "You come here often?"

"Pretty often," said Jere.

"Come see me sometime. I'll take you around." Jere followed him out. O'Reilly fastened the gate with a heavy padlock. "If you're ever interested in volunteering, we're always looking for people."

"I'll think about that, thanks," said Jere. He walked away, headed toward the Rain Forest House. He went in the building and wandered past the exhibits without seeing them.

The bird man was here. There were so many places to hide, so much space not watched over by anyone, and groves of trees, and rocks, and miles of fence perimeter smothered in overgrown shrubbery. The bird man could even be living here, though it would be hard to camp out without being found. In any case, he was close by and coming back to the zoo.

How could he do that without being seen by the people at the zoo who knew him? Maybe he came in disguise. There were so many odd-looking people around, he'd never stick out in a crowd. But some zoo staff person would notice if he stayed in the birdcage a long time. Maybe he came in at night. Climbed over the fence somewhere. He wouldn't have to worry about being recognized then, except maybe by a duck or two.

By nine o'clock on Sunday night, Jere figured Avery was probably back from her weekend at Aunt Diane's, so he called her.

"Guess what? I did remember the whole thing. I finally remembered."

"Oh. *Oh!* You mean that guy? Wow, that's something! Wait'll I tell my mom. She kept saying you'd probably come up with it sooner or later."

"Don't say anything yet! Is your mom around where she can hear you?"

"She's taking a shower."

"Are you ready for this? I went to the zoo, and I saw this trail of crumbs in the flight cage. These crushed-up cheese things. Al Watkins eats those. He's still around."

"No, no, he can't be."

"He is."

"A trail of crumbs? Sounds like Hansel and Gretel. Random, Jere, random."

"He was there. I know he was. He went back to the cage. Maybe he goes a lot. Maybe he misses the ducks—you know, he's used to taking care of them."

Avery let out a shrill laugh.

"Listen, I'm going to hide out in the zoo when it closes and see if he comes."

"Jere! Are you crazy? You're getting like this obsession or something."

"No, really. We could follow him if we're careful, and then find out where he's hiding. We tell the police. They arrest him."

"We?"

"I was just thinking two against one is better odds."

"No."

"Come on, Avery."

"Take Officer Bradley, why don't you?"

"She'd never let a kid do this. And he'd know if police were there. He picks up on stuff like that."

"How do you know what he picks up on?"

"Look. If we hide and don't move, he can't see us, and he won't be expecting anybody, so he'll be off his guard."

"Speaking of guard, why hasn't some night watchman caught him?"

"He probably knows when the guards go around."

"You mean you're literally going to hide? Where? Under a rock?"

"There's plenty of places behind bushes and all. When they close up, they can't check everywhere. Especially not outside."

Avery was silent. Then she gave a long sigh. "You know, I wasn't going to say anything, but I did think I might've seen him again. Once at night. Out in front, a couple of weeks ago. Everyone got into such a *state* before."

"It's got to be him, don't you see? He thinks he's safe, that nobody knows where he is."

"Well, there's no way my mom's letting me out on a school night, not any more this year."

"So we'll go Friday. Tell your mom we're going to a movie and getting pizza, something like that, and I'll say the same thing."

"What makes you think he'll come that night?"

"No way to know."

"And what're you going to say when the night watchman turns up and shines his flashlight into your eyes?"

"What's the worst that could happen? We're not vandalizing anything or hurting any animals. Just act like it was a dumb prank. They won't put us in jail."

"I was going to go shopping this Friday."

He waited.

"Let me think about it by myself. This is too scary."

Jere hung up. Twenty minutes later, he grabbed the phone after the first ring.

"I guess I will," said Avery. "But if anything messes up, Jere, you're really going to be in for it."

"It won't. Trust me, it won't."

But by Friday, he had thought of all sorts of ways it could mess up. First, there was no reason to assume the bird man would show up. Second, if he did come, he could have a gun with him. Third, the bird man had to be a certified crazy person, in which case common sense didn't apply. There was no predicting what he would do. But Jere wanted to see him, had to find him; there was no way he could stop.

*   *   *   *   *

They had to get there at least an hour before closing time; that was when the zoo stopped selling admission tickets.

"Did you eat anything?" Jere asked.

Avery nodded. "And I brought some candy bars. In case we're here for a long time." She wore her backpack over a fleece jacket.

It felt so good to have her walking beside him again. They circled the entire zoo, looking for a hiding place. There was no one at all in the Hooves and Horns exhibit. But it was on the opposite side of the zoo from the birds, and to get where they needed to be, once the zoo closed, they'd have to cross the huge open space in the center or sneak halfway around the edge of the whole zoo.

By quarter of five, it was nearly dark, and the last families were heading out of the gates. Jere walked deliberately past the entrance to the flight cage and down a hill, hoping he looked as if he had an official job to do. He went around behind a metal shed that was padlocked shut. A narrow space was cleared beside the shed, and beyond it scraggly shrubbery obscured the outside fence. Avery stepped neatly around the corner of the shed after Jere, and they both sat down. The ground was cold and gritty. If anyone found them now, they could say they were just talking and had forgotten about the time.

It grew darker quickly. In the distance Jere heard a voice calling, "Closing time! Closing, all!"

Nobody came near the shed. Jere didn't hear any voices after the man stopped calling out. It wasn't like a museum, after all, where they can check every corner before they lock up.

Cars started, drove away. A door closed somewhere. A pair of headlights suddenly came on right in their faces; they ducked their heads, and the lights backed away, turned to the side, drove off.

Now there were no human voices at all, but they began to hear animals on every side. They sat without moving. Jere's jacket sleeve was pulled up, and he could see his watch face glowing green in the dark. Twenty minutes past five.

"How long do we have to sit here?" Avery whispered. He could feel her arm shivering. Something crunched a few yards to the right of the shed. Jere grabbed Avery's wrist and motioned to be still. Loud crunching footsteps, keys jingling, someone singing. Jere leaned around the corner of the shed. Under the sparse walkway lights, a tall man wearing a uniform walked heavily away from them toward the Rain Forest House.

"It's the watchman. Now's our chance, while he's gone."

Their rustling seemed loud as they delicately picked their way through the stretch of woods to the fence near the back of the flight cage. They stood there for a moment, looking for a place to hide. The black wires of the cage arched high above them, visible against the evening sky.

"Let's look for a place near one of the gates," Jere whispered.

Avery nodded.

They climbed a slope beside the cage on their hands and feet, leaves and stones slipping away behind them. Then Jere could hear the watchman singing again. "He's coming back. Down, quick, by that tree." They scrambled back a few yards to the other side of a crooked pine tree with a thick trunk. They huddled down and curled themselves over, then froze. The asphalt walkway was well above their heads.

"Oh my darling, oh my darling...," sang the night watchman. Tromp, tromp, tromp. Jere waited for the sound of unlocking. Nothing. Then a fat white beam of light shot past them, circled below, was snapped off.

"You are lost and gone forever," he sang, and Jere heard him walk away. The man coughed, then picked up his song.

"How long till he comes back?" whispered Avery.

"Who knows?"

It was a whole hour till he came back on his next round. He was singing a different song this time. Jere and Avery had been standing, lifting up their feet and bending their knees, trying to stretch out the cramps in their legs. It seemed as if they had been crouching there or wriggling around trying to find a new position for about six hours. It was so boring, Jere forgot about being nervous.

"Down!" Avery hissed at him. They were getting better at instantly shrinking into balls. Though he had ducked his head down, Jere kept his eyes open and looked off to the side. The flashlight beam swept by again. Apparently, the watchman didn't go into the flight cage, just inspected it from the outside. "We three kings of Orient are!" came his hearty voice.

At the end of another hour, Jere was aching all over. The watchman was due back, but he didn't come. Maybe he didn't go around every hour. Maybe he changed his schedule so it wasn't predictable.

Avery slipped off her backpack and took out a Snickers and handed it to Jere. He was starving, and he ate it in three bites. Avery ate one, gave him another. The candy warmed him up for a few minutes.

Another hour dragged by. No night watchman, no bird man. Jere hadn't counted on how long he'd have to wait. "I'm not staying here all night," whispered Avery, sounding cross.

At ten-thirty, they heard steps again on the asphalt path, no singing this time. But the person made a lot of noise—keys jangling, feet tromping. The footsteps stopped. Then a metal gate opened with a screech, clanged shut. Jere pushed himself partway to his feet. A light swept around inside the flight cage. "It's a different guy," he whispered.

This watchman took five minutes, strolling to the end of the walkway and back, swinging his light from the ground to the trees and down again. Jere and Avery ducked out of sight as he came back to the entrance. They heard the padlock snap shut. The man went away. They stood up and were shaking out their arms and legs when Avery suddenly froze, pulled at Jere. Someone else was coming along the path, without making a sound. They dropped down. There was a very small noise of metal scraping metal, then nothing.

Chapter TEN

Jere crawled and wriggled to the top of the slope. He raised his head but couldn't see into the flight cage. He slowly straightened up and moved toward the entrance. There was no way he could conceal himself, but the cage was full of shadows from nearby trees, and if he went slowly, he wouldn't be so noticeable in the dark.

The gate was closed, the open padlock hanging from one side. Jere pushed the gate open and slipped through, with Avery right behind him. They moved a few yards along the elevated walkway without a sound.

Jere's eyes were already used to the dark, but it took a moment to make out the patterns of shadows within the cage, dark lying across dark.

There he was. He was standing where Jere had seen him before, on the ground level by the pond. He had his back to them, and he was talking in a low voice to the sleeping ducks, who floated on the surface like feathery footballs. Jere felt Avery slip her hand into his, and that's how they were standing when the bird man turned around. He must have heard something, the smallest wrong noise. Jere could see his face turn up toward them. He was still talking in a low voice. Suddenly, the man ran toward the base of the walkway, swung himself up, climbed over the handrail, and stopped short. Jere and Avery stood facing him with their hands linked. The man began to walk toward them, fumbling in his pocket with one hand.

Something swooped over their heads with a rush of wide wings, heavy beats against the night air.

Jere's heart was pounding, and his legs were shaking. Why had he ever thought of doing this? He wished he was anywhere else in the world. This fellow was a madman. He could walk right up to them and shoot them. If Jere and Avery tried to run, he could shoot them in the back. His clothes and jacket were baggy; he could be hiding a gun. If only he would say something to them.

Avery let go of Jere's hand and bolted for the gate. The bird man caught up with her in two steps, yanked on her arm, and sent her sprawling against the walkway guardrail. He was at the gate, out of it, then turned and snapped the padlock shut. "You should have kept away," he said in a high, pinched voice, like a child trying not to cry, and the next minute he had gone off the side, down through the leaves and brush. They heard rustling noises for a few seconds, a pause, a thump that must have been him landing outside the zoo fence, running footsteps that quickly faded to nothing.

Avery got to her feet slowly. "We're really in it now," she said. She was trembling all over.

"At least we know he's still here," said Jere.

"We're the ones that are still here."

There was a noise of beating wings again, and from somewhere high up in the cage a huge bird came toward them, swerved at the last moment, and banked steeply up into the top of the cage.

"What was that?" Avery said, whirling around.

It came again from a different direction. They both dropped down, threw their arms over their heads.

"Guess we're in its territory," said Jere.

"Is there any other way out of here? Any, like, fire exit?"

"We could get under this walkway. At least it can't dive-bomb us under there."

They scrambled toward the end of the walkway, where the ground sloped up closely underneath. "Watch it! Here it comes," Jere shouted. There was no time to go over the rail. Avery sprang toward the exit. She snatched open the inner wire door, and they both jumped inside and slammed the door shut. The bird hovered close to the wire, its yellow eye focused on them, then circled away.

Jere looked around at the wire enclosure. "I'd rather have the night watchman get us than that thing."

"What if what's-his-name comes back first?"

"Guess we better start making noise."

The police took Jere and Avery to the local station and had them sit on a wooden bench. Jere kept asking them to call Officer Bradley before they called his parents, and finally they did. Luckily, she had weekend duty, and she came over even though it was past midnight.

"We'll search the zoo immediately," she said. "Bring in anyone not authorized to be on the zoo grounds." She spoke to two police officers leaning on a counter nearby, and they immediately straightened up. One began radioing for cars, and the other ran for the door. "I don't know what we should do with you," she said, turning to Jere and Avery. "Can you explain yourselves?"

"I had a feeling he was coming back to the zoo," said Jere.

"A feeling?"

"I went back and saw some crumbs in the flight cage, crumbs from stuff he likes to eat, and I just knew he had been there."

"You should have come to us. We could have staked out the cage ourselves. We had plainclothes officers at the zoo."

"I guess so." He didn't care if he looked thoughtless or stupid. It was easier to go along with that.

"This man is suspected of having shot someone."

"I know," said Jere.

His parents and Avery's mother arrived at nearly the same moment, ran into the station, and clutched at their children. Avery burst into tears as her mother hugged her and patted her back; Jere's father kept saying, "Jere has gotten carried away with this business, just carried away." His mother put her hands over his and squeezed. His parents stayed on one side of the room and Avery's mother stayed on the other; each side gave the other that polite look that meant, I know my child is in trouble, and of course we will deal with it, but it's basically your kid's fault.

"You'll have to bear with me. You can't go home yet," said Bradley. "Everybody sit down, please. There're extra chairs you can pull up. I need you two to tell me everything you remember about what happened. What was the man wearing? Did you see where he went after he locked you in the cage?"

They spent half an hour going over the details. Jere kept thinking, This isn't going to do any good. You're not going to find him by knowing what he was wearing. In fact, you're not going to find him at all by looking for him. He'll come out on his own. When he thinks it's safe, he'll come out on his own.

"I'll talk this over with the zoo," Bradley finished up, "but my inclination is to advise them not to press charges. For now, we'll release you both into your parents' custody." Jere and Avery nodded. "To state the obvious, this isn't a rational person. You think you see him, you call me that very minute. Holy cow, Jere! I'm so glad you're both okay. Don't do this to me again!"

The Robisons were silent on the drive home.

"Grounded," said Avery. "Big-time. She won't even say how long. She was ripping, once she got over being shook-up. How about you?"

"Same thing. No social life, all that. I thought they'd make me drop basketball, but they just said I have to go to every practice. This is the first time in three days they've let me use the phone. My dad just about told me not to talk to anybody at all, but he can't exactly monitor that."

"Hmm. I don't suppose they'd go for us doing homework together." Avery gave a laugh.

"I don't suppose they would."

"Where do you think that creep went? Ugh. He's somewhere, you know? Did you see the way he looked at us?"

"He knew who we were."

"Don't say that!" Avery squealed. "And then when he grabbed my arm— His hand was like this strong, I don't know, iron grip—even though he looks sort of weak, maybe because his clothes are all dirty and messy. He smelled bad!"

They both began to laugh.

"Wait a sec. Somebody's at the door. My mom's at another condo meeting. I have to get it. It's probably some neighbor." She dropped the phone with a clatter.

Jere waited. It felt so good to talk to her again—it seemed like the first time in days that his stomach knots had untied themselves.

"Nobody," said Avery.

Neither one of them said anything.

"Now I'm nervous," she said. "I don't want there to be something out there that knocks and goes away. I wish my mom didn't have to keep going to these condo meetings. Here I am alone. Can you come over? Even though you can't?"

"My dad would lock me up for a year. Seriously."

"Yep. He would. Oh well... The meeting's not supposed to last that long. It's about security. Get a grip, Avery." She gave an enormous sigh. "Maybe it was just Kyle."

Jere's stomach did a three-sixty. "What's he doing there?"

"Didn't I tell you? His uncle moved into my building. Way last September. He's actually asked my mom out a couple of times. Kyle's uncle, I mean. Sometimes Kyle comes over and hangs out at his uncle's."

"Oh." Jere felt a rocket of glee. "Oh."

"He's such a goof-off," said Avery.

"Always been like that," said Jere.

"But I doubt if that was him. He doesn't knock, for one thing; he just kind of hollers. And I haven't seen him since his uncle stopped coming on to my mom. Basically a jerk."

"Right."

"So who was it?"

"If you're so worried, why don't you just go to where the meeting is?"

"I don't even want to walk down the hall by myself. Jere, I'm quaking. This is ridiculous."

"Call security. There's that guy down there at the desk, isn't there?"

"It's too embarrassing. Oh, no, wait. I think I heard it again. There're more knocks. Man, I'm about to go out the back door."

"Look—is your front door locked? Go lock it."

She dropped the phone again.

He couldn't go over to Avery's without okaying it with his parents—that would really be the end. He still had to live with them for three more years before he went away to college.

Avery came back to the phone. "I bolted it," she said. "I didn't even look through the peephole." Her voice sounded steadier. "I wish you were the one who lived in my building instead of Kyle's uncle. Wait a sec—there's my mom. She's calling me from the hall— she can't get in. Oh Lordy, hooray. Talk to you later."

He felt lonely after they hung up. His father was working late; his mother had said she was going to the library. He wished he did live in Avery's building. And if they weren't at the stage of being in love, they could just be like cousins, hang out together. He liked Avery's mother a lot. She probably thought he was an idiot now, but she'd get over it. They could have meals together sometimes, like with the Scotts. That sort of thing.

He lay back on his bed, put his hands under his head, stared at the ceiling. There used to be a pattern of cracks around the light fixture that he could turn into pictures. But his room had been repainted last summer.

He just wanted to think about nothing for a while; he especially didn't want to think about the bird man, hiding out wherever he was. Jere couldn't turn his mind another way, though. He never really stopped thinking about him. The fellow had had such a funny look on his face that night when he saw them on the walkway. He looked afraid.

"You should have kept away," he'd said, sounding all upset. Jere hadn't liked that—it was as if the man wasn't surprised to see them there. It was too close for comfort; maybe the man didn't recognize any boundary between them; maybe Jere and Avery had become part of what existed in his head—whatever that was.

Jere felt a shiver ripple across his shoulders. He sat up, reached for the phone, dialed Avery's number. It rang four times, and then the answering machine came on. He stood up. Now *he* was starting to get scared. It was stupid. She could be taking a shower, or maybe she went out with her mom to the drugstore. But he had a bad feeling about it. So be sensible, he told himself. He dialed the police station and asked for Officer Bradley. That's what she'd said to do, after all.

"She's gone home. Sorry. Anybody else who can help you?"

"I don't think so."

"What's the problem?"

"Oh, I—just worried about something—nothing actually happened. Officer Bradley knows me. So, do you have her home number?"

"Can't give that to you—we're not allowed to. She'll be in in the morning. Whyn't you try her then?"

"Okay." He pressed down the button, tried Avery again. Answering machine.

The front door opened and closed, and his mother called hello up the stairs. There went his chance to leave on his own. He went downstairs.

"Mom, look, about this being on probation, or whatever it is—"

His mother raised her hand. "We're not changing it."

"Does it count if you take me over to Avery's house?"

"*Now*, you mean?"

"I was just talking to her on the phone, and now she

isn't answering, and she thought someone was at her door a while ago when she was there by herself."

"Haven't we had enough running around in the dark?"

"I can't help it. She sounded scared. I just want to go over there and make sure it really was her mother and she's okay."

"Jere, we can't drop everything every time somebody doesn't answer the phone."

"The last time I had a hunch about something, it turned out to be right."

"Yes, and you ended up in a terrible situation." His mother paused and looked as if this thought had doubled back and taken her by surprise. "Oh, all right. I'll take you over there, but I'm coming in with you."

They stood at the inner door to Avery's building and buzzed number 7B. "Who is it?" Mrs. Cummings's voice was blurry over the intercom.

"Mrs. Robison and Jere. Can we come up?"

The buzzer sounded. They took the elevator up, and Mrs. Cummings opened the door. Avery was standing behind her.

"Is everything all right here?" Jere's mother asked.

"Of course," said Mrs. Cummings crisply.

"You didn't answer the phone; I didn't know what was going on," said Jere.

Mrs. Cummings glanced at their answering machine, which was blinking. "We went downstairs to talk to the guard about some knocking noises Avery heard, that's all."

"This business is nerve-racking, isn't it?" said Jere's mother, suddenly sounding warmer.

"I'm on edge all the time," Mrs. Cummings agreed with a tentative smile. "Well, look, since you're here, do you want to sit down for a few minutes? I could make you a cup of tea."

"Oh, don't go to the trouble," said Jere's mother. "It's late. But I'm glad we came and there's nothing wrong."

"So what did the knocks turn out to be?" asked Jere.

"Dunno," said Avery. "They don't vacuum the halls at night, so it wasn't the custodian."

"I'm wondering if it was an elevator noise," said Mrs. Cummings, "something you hear all the time but don't notice till you're suddenly paying attention to everything."

"I'm getting hyper all right," said Avery.

As Jere and his mother passed the security guard on their way out, he gave them a nod of recognition.

They got into the car. "That seems like a good building," said his mother. "I think I like Avery's mother."

"She's really nice," said Jere. "Maybe she likes you, too."

His mother gave him a look that said, Why on earth wouldn't she? "Not exactly a wild-goose chase, but I wonder how long we'll go on doing this sort of thing," she went on, backing out of the parking place. "Probably till they find him," she answered herself.

"Right," said Jere mechanically. Not a wild-goose chase. What was that anyway? Where did people get these little phrases? More like a wild-duck chase. He watched a row of parked cars flick past in the dark—everyone was home now, snug in their beds. Al Watkins had to be sleeping somewhere, snug in a bed or not. If he had been actually living at the zoo, he'd never go back there now. They'd be watching the flight cage all the time. He was probably too smart to do that, anyhow. Too easy to be trapped if he was discovered.

"You coming in?" His mother had parked and was sitting behind the steering wheel, waiting for him to get out so she could lock the car doors.

Chapter ELEVEN

"It wasn't the elevator," Avery said the next day.

"No?" Jere asked. "No," he agreed. They were walking from math to Spanish.

"What if it was him? Maybe he's been walking up and down our street and going in and out of the buildings and looking at the mailboxes. But how would he know my name? Shoot. I didn't sleep all night." Avery looked as if she hadn't slept for a lot longer than that. She was white, and her face had a pinched look. Her hair hung limp and mussed instead of swinging out around her ears the way it usually did.

Jere knew he was going to put his arm around her, which he'd never done before. He felt himself do it—yep, there went his arm. Had he landed too heavily on her shoulder? Where should his hand go? Squeeze her shoulder? Just droop down near her arm? His fingers were so limp, just dangling there, he was scared he'd grab the wrong part of her. She leaned against him as

they walked, put her hand up over his, and gave his
hand a squeeze of comfort.

She was waiting for him by the gym after last period.
"Going to basketball?" she asked.

"Got to."

"Maybe I'll stay and watch."

She sat in the bleachers, with her notebook open—
Jere guessed she wanted to look like she was doing
homework. She was still there when he came out of the
locker room. She didn't ask him outright, just gave him
a miserable, pleading smile. "Mom's at work till six," she
said as they started out the main school door. "Nobody's
home in my building till five-thirty."

"Nobody?"

"Hardly anybody. A couple of old ladies."

They waited for the bus together. "I can always say
practice was late," said Jere.

They got off at Avery's stop and walked quickly up
the block toward her building. It was only four o'clock,
and light still lingered, but the afternoon had a bleak,
wintry quality. The storefronts seemed garish; a set of
tiny Christmas lights blinked around the window of a
fancy-food shop.

The security guard buzzed them in. Avery's apartment smelled good. "My mom baked some cookies last night before she went to bed." Wire cooling racks covered with cookies in the shape of stars and bells were scattered around the kitchen. "We can have a couple. I'm supposed to put them away. And do a load of laundry."

Jere bit into one of the stars. It was barely soft in the middle, just the way he liked them.

Avery pulled out two empty cookie tins and began lining them with pieces of waxed paper. "You can do this one," she said, handing him one of the tins. He arranged layers of cookies between more pieces of waxed paper. He fitted the top back on.

"Now what?" he said.

"Laundry."

She went into her mother's bedroom and brought out a basket of towels and sheets. "If you want to start your homework so they won't get so mad, you can do it here." She turned on a hanging lamp over the kitchen table. He got his notebook and his math assignment and spread them out.

"I feel so much better with you here," said Avery, and she gave him one of her best smiles as she went out the door.

Jere shuffled the papers around—it wasn't so easy to

settle down in someone else's space. And then he heard someone knock. He jumped to his feet. "Who is it?" he hollered in a wave of fright.

"It's me. I forgot my key!" Avery stood there with the basketful of dirty laundry.

She took a key from a hook in the kitchen and turned, chewing her lip. "Listen, want to come along?" He nodded. She closed the apartment door, tested the knob to be sure it was locked. They took the elevator to the basement.

As soon as they stepped into the laundry room, Jere knew something was wrong, and in the next instant he realized it was too late to do anything about it. A narrow door behind the hot-water tanks was open. He got a glimpse of a small room with a pile of rags in it, and he smelled something stale and pungent, and then he saw the bird man. The bird man had already seen them. He was standing just inside the hidden room, right by the door frame, and he did have a gun. He quickly walked around them, closed the laundry room door, and bolted it.

He pointed the gun at them, waved it back and forth to signal them to move toward each other. He was holding the gun with a steady hand, but his face was agitated, as if conflicting thoughts were pushing each other through his head. He didn't say anything.

It was four-thirty. Avery had said practically nobody was home in her building till five-thirty at the earliest, so unless the security guard decided to check the basement, they were going to be spending a long time with Al Watkins. Maybe Avery's mother would come home early. But could she figure out where they were? They hadn't left behind anything to make her think of calling the police. Jere couldn't help staring at the gun. It looked so small, compared to what it could do.

The bird man was muttering something. Did he believe he was talking to someone? Jere didn't know whether to pretend he hadn't heard or act as if he thought the man was speaking to him or just wait. Out of the corner of his eye, he could see Avery shaking. She dropped one end of the laundry basket and let out a little cry. All the laundry tumbled out onto the floor.

The bird man went stiff. He glared at her, said something to himself. She stood frozen and shivering. "You be quiet," he said to her. "You followed me here."

"No, no, I didn't know you were here." Avery's voice was high-pitched and shaking.

"You live here," Watkins said.

Avery nodded.

He turned to Jere. "What about you?"

Jere's impulse was to tell the truth, as if that would placate the man. "Across town, over on Hiller Park," he said.

"Hiller Park," Watkins repeated. He moved the gun from side to side, now aiming it at Jere, now at Avery. He was sweating.

Jere's mind raced, panicky and aimless, like a bumper car at an amusement park. Just slow everything down, he told himself. Slow. *Slow.* He remembered O'Reilly at the zoo talking about handling birds. Careful and slow. Nothing to startle them. Say something, Jere told himself, anything. Talk about birds.

"I guess you must know a lot about birds," he forced out. Watkins gave him a surprised look. "That's where we met you the first time—I don't know if you remember. It was at the zoo, with the birds." *I don't know if you remember?* That was rich.

The man's face seemed to calm down. Jere was about to say, *We both like birds,* when he stopped himself. Better not say anything about *we.* "I'm sort of interested in them myself, but you know a lot more than I do. That's why we were there that night, went to see them, you know, sleeping—"

"Shut up," said the man.

Jere swallowed and nodded. It seemed like half an

hour had gone by, but the big clock on the wall showed it had been less than five minutes.

The bird man began to speak to Avery in a hoarse voice: "I wasn't feeding them. You walk up and say that. I wasn't. You know that."

"No, no, you weren't, yes," Avery stammered.

"You walk up and say that and now something terrible has to happen." He waved his hand toward the little room behind the tanks. Avery stared at him as if she was trying to decipher his gesture, but it was perfectly clear what he wanted her to do.

"Go in there?" she said, her voice tight and breathless.

He nodded and waved the gun at her. She went into the room.

Watkins didn't follow her.

"Sit down," he said to Jere. "There."

Jere dropped onto a bench beside the wall. He glanced around the room. A couple of plastic jugs of detergent sat in the far corner, and on top of one of the washing machines was a white container of bleach. No way to tell if it was full or empty. He didn't know how he'd do anyhow, if he tried a lightning-quick move. Better to slow everything down. His heart was beating so fast, he felt giddy. Good thing he was sitting down.

"Now wait," said the man. He stood well away from Jere, treading on one of Avery's mother's towels. With his free hand, he pulled a yellow packet from his pants pocket, opened it with his teeth, shook some of the contents into his mouth, and crunched noisily. A salty, cheesy smell reached Jere's nose. The man appeared to think of something. A look of surprise crossed his face, and he said something unintelligible to himself.

Jere made himself stay quiet. Don't talk.

"She followed me here," he said to Jere. "She's been looking for me. All this time."

Jere said nothing, just pressed his quaking hands around his knees to keep them still.

"She told the police. The police were asking questions. 'Where were you ten years ago? Have you ever been to Hiller Park?' But everyone forgot. It was gone. Nobody knew. Nobody remembered."

Hiller Park? Jere hadn't thought of the bird man knowing the name of the place. But of course he would know it.

He was going on, talking to some invisible listener. "So long ago, so long, no one can remember such a long time, and then it didn't happen really. The doctors came and fixed her, didn't they? Isn't that her in there? The police came to the zoo and were asking and asking. And now I have to remember. And I shouldn't have to. I shouldn't."

He suddenly let out a horrible sound. He began to cry, but it wasn't like any crying Jere had ever heard— more like chaotic noises, half shouts, half barks from deep in his chest. "I didn't really do it. It just happened. But I always have my gun. She told me not to feed them that *junk*. I wasn't even feeding them! What did she know? Nothing. *Nothing.* So, *bang!* Don't tell me, not me, not about ducks. And nobody saw—that's because it wasn't my fault. Except a baby, but he was only playing, playing, way up high in his window. Nobody heard. Nobody came out of their houses. I walked away real slow. It was dark, you know. Nobody saw me except a baby."

Jere didn't make a sound.

Suddenly, Watkins's crying noises stopped, and his face changed from being twisted up to blank. "Now it's going to be a secret again." He went into the little room. "Lie down," he said to Avery. Jere froze. A hot, sick feeling flooded his stomach. He couldn't see around the wall, but he heard a small rustling sound. "Not like that. Curl up," said the man. More rustling. "You kept following me. And now I have to do it again, *all over again!*"

Jere's eardrums swelled against the silence, listening for a click of the gun, the smallest rustle of clothing.

Watkins came back out. Jere's stomach gave a heave; he was afraid he might throw up.

"I have my plans," he said to Jere. "They told me what to do."

Slow. "What's that?"

"Don't get in my way."

"No, no, I won't."

"They told me everything to do."

"Yes," said Jere.

"Yes," the man said. "This room in here is mine. No one else's. It's a secret."

Jere swallowed. His throat was so dry, it practically stuck together. He didn't know whether he should agree with the man, flatter him, or say nothing. There was no way of telling if he was going to shoot Avery. He might step around the corner and fire the gun, or he might not. And how long would it take him to connect Jere with Hiller Park? "Secrets—" Jere croaked. "Secrets are important."

"Sometimes," snapped the man. "Don't tell me about it." He ate some more from the yellow packet. "She knows." He nodded toward the room where Avery was. "That's why she tried to keep me away from the birds."

"She wasn't trying—"

"Yes she was!" he shouted. He waved the gun and looked upset. A muffled crying sound came from the hidden room. "And now she's sorry," said the man. "Now it has to happen again."

Jere shook his head, but he was afraid that if he spoke out loud, he would set Watkins off. Jere knew he could jump on him right now—he would have one chance to do that—but the gun would be sure to fire, and probably Watkins wouldn't stop once he had fired it. Maybe it wasn't too late for him to change his mind. Maybe he wasn't ready to kill again. But how could you tell?

The laundry room doorknob rattled and began to turn back and forth, and then someone pressed against the door. Most days, it was probably never locked. The bird man saw it, too.

"Who's that?" he snapped.

The knob rattled and turned.

"Tell them something," he said to Jere, and he stepped into the little room. "I'll be listening. Tell them what they want to hear."

Jere stood up. He saw through the doorway that Watkins was standing over Avery, aiming the gun at her head, while she crouched in a ball at his feet. Watkins pushed the door nearly shut.

Jere shakily drew back the bolt on the laundry room door and opened it. A tiny, frail-looking old woman stood there with a pink laundry bag. At her feet was a box of Tide. "You scared me!" she said. "This door is never locked!"

"Just security," said Jere.

"Oh, of course. All this trouble we're having. But who are you? You're not security. You don't live in this building."

"No, I'm checking the machines, that's all. They're broken."

"Which ones? Didn't Mr. Costello take care of that? He always does that. You don't look to me like you belong here, young man. Where's your uniform if you're here to fix the washing machines?" She took a few steps into the room. "Why is that door back there open? Whose laundry is that all over the floor?"

"Nothing to worry about," said Jere, and he pushed her, pink bag and all, back outside the laundry room. "Just let me get to my work. I can't be interrupted— that's why I locked the door," he said loudly. Then he mouthed at her, once, *Help.* She pulled away from him, and he slammed the door in her face. He slid the bolt with a *whang,* pretended to struggle with it, managed to slide it back partway. He turned. Al Watkins had reappeared.

He'd had no time, and the lady had been rattled. He wished he had thought of making her really mad; then she'd be sure to go for help.

The bird man wandered along the row of dryers. Jere started to cross the room toward his bench, and the bird man shouted, "Stop there. Don't move till I tell you to."

Jere froze, and now for the first time a wave of anger moved through him. He didn't feel like being shouted at anymore. It seemed as if they had been here for hours, though the clock had dragged around only twenty-five minutes. The next instant, the terror returned, engulfing his anger so fast that he lost his breath. If he kept going back and forth like this, he'd die of fright before he ever got shot.

"I was just going to shut that door," Jere said. "So the room will stay hidden. And safe for you. So it'll be a secret." Maybe he shouldn't have said the word *secret.*

"Oh, yes. That's in the plans. I'll do it. You stay there." Jere held his breath. The bird man walked over to the hidden room, groped around the wall for the light switch, flicked it off, and pulled the door shut. Then he suddenly whirled around to face Jere. Fortunately, Jere hadn't moved a muscle. *Act reliable. Act like you're his ally.* He glanced away from the bird man and saw the latch on the hidden door turn a quarter of the way around. It made a click. Jere tried to cover the noise by scraping his feet. The latch moved the next quarter turn, so it looked the same as it had before. The door was locked from inside. Avery was safe for now.

"What's that?" The man cocked his head. Jere heard a siren, faint and far away. *Please be coming here,* he thought. *Please.*

The siren stopped.

Now the bird man seemed agitated again.

"You told them I was here, didn't you?" he said to Jere.

Jere shook his head. His heart was hammering, suffocating him.

Watkins leaned close to Jere's face. "But you did! What did you tell the old woman? She'll tell! Is that the police? Listen!" Jere heard nothing but the bird man's labored breathing. If the police were coming, they must have turned their sirens off.

"Police asking questions. 'Where were you ten years

ago?' So I had to hide. 'Have you ever been to Hiller Park? Where were you ten years ago?' Why did the police ask me? No one knew about it. No one saw. A baby can't tell."

What if Watkins recognized him at last? What if Jere's face looked the same now as when he was four? Some kids looked like themselves from their first little baby pictures till they graduated from high school. Jere could hardly breathe.

"Can he? *A baby can't tell!*" Watkins stood over Jere. "Where were you ten years ago...." He was talking to himself more than to Jere, and then his gaze shifted to Jere in a distracted way, and their eyes locked. Something in Jere's face must have given him away— some shift in his expression, some way his eyes involuntarily changed.

"Wait—that's where you said. *You*—you told!" He stepped sideways and put both hands around the handle of his gun and pointed it at Jere's face.

Three loud blows shook the laundry room door. The bird man whipped around to see. Harsh shouts came from the hall. "Open up in there! Police!"

There was panic in Watkins's face. His features were agitated, his face so contorted Jere could barely see his eyes. He searched for Jere's arm, yanked him up. Avery was right—he was incredibly strong and agile, despite his sloppy appearance. He pressed the barrel of the gun into the back of Jere's neck. "Tell them to go away, or I'll kill you."

"Go away or he'll kill me," Jere shouted.

"Open up!" a man was yelling.

The bird man grunted in frustration, pulled Jere this way and that. Jere made himself stay flexible. Once someone had said that if you're in a car accident, you should go limp. Now he was getting shoved over near the washing machines.

"Who's in there? Answer!"

"Answer," ordered the bird man.

Someone rattled the doorknob and pushed on the door. It gave a bit around the frame. The bolt slipped back a little.

"Stop! He has a gun!" Jere shouted.

The shaking of the door stopped.

"They can't hear what I'm saying," said Jere.

"So open and tell them." The bird man walked him over to the door, one hand on his shoulder, the other pressing the gun into Jere's back.

Jere slid the bolt back. *Slow, go slow.* "I'm opening the door," he hollered. "Don't do anything. He has a gun." Jere slowly pulled the door open. Three uniformed police officers stood there, and way behind them was the old lady.

"What's going on?" asked one officer.

Nobody answered.

"Get your hands up, way up in the air!" said Watkins, his eyes darting from one man to the next.

"All right, buddy, take it easy," said the second police officer. They put their hands up. The old lady was gone.

"Can we talk this over?" the third officer said. "Would you put down your gun and we can all talk together?"

"You're not telling the truth!" shrieked the bird man. "You don't want to talk! You'll lock me up!"

The officers looked at one another.

"We don't even know you," said the first one again. His voice was amazingly low and soothing. "Let's talk first. I'm sure you can put that gun down. Can you put it on the floor? We can't talk with a gun in the middle of the conversation."

"This is a trick!"

"We'll listen to you. Tell us what's happening. I promise we will listen."

"Who is this young fellow with you?" asked the second officer. "Let him leave, and then we can talk."

The bird man began to tremble. "No. No, no, no." He began to drag Jere backward. The three officers didn't move, but their expressions changed, and one of them said something. A walkie-talkie went off.

"Can't we sit down and talk?" the third officer suggested again, as if nothing out of the ordinary was happening. "We've got plenty of time." The walkie-talkie spat out static and a voice they could all understand this time: "Dispatch forty-seven. Do you read? Answer, please. We assume you still have a forty-seven."

The bird man was shaking and yanking Jere toward the hot-water tanks, and then Jere, half-staggering backward, caught his shoe in one of the towels on the floor and accidentally stepped on the bird man's foot. The man stumbled. He took a couple of clumsy steps backward and the gun left Jere's back. Jere lunged for the jug of bleach, grabbed it, swung it around, and smashed it right in the bird man's face.

Jere threw himself backward, stumbled, and fell toward the bench against the other wall. A flash of white light came from the bird man's direction, and one other sharp noise rang off the cement-block walls. Jere was on the floor, and so was the bird man, crumpled against a hot-water tank, with red blood on the front of his clothes. Then all three officers were in the room, and Jere heard someone in the hall let out a cry: "He's dead! Oh my God, he's dead!"

Chapter TWELVE

Avery wouldn't come out until she heard Jere's voice telling her it was okay.

When she opened the door and stumbled toward him, a stench from the rotten food and rags came out, too. Now there were even more police officers in the laundry room. Two of them rushed into the hidden room; a couple of others were kneeling by the bird man, pressing down on his chest. "Radio for paramedics," one of them shouted. "He's still breathing." Another siren sounded close by.

"It was horrible!" Avery was crying. Jere put his arms around her skinny shoulder blades, and she burrowed into his chest with the top of her head.

"It's over now," said an officer. "It's over now."

"Where's my mom? I want my mother!" Avery said between sobs.

"She might be outside. They've cordoned off the building. Let's go out and see. You live here, too, son?"

An ambulance crew ran into the room, pulling out emergency equipment as they came.

Avery and Jere and two officers took the elevator to the first floor and went outside. Jere felt strangely numb, as if he were floating. A crowd had gathered at the foot of the steps to the entrance. "Is there a Mrs. Cummings here?" one of the officers called out. The people passed her name along: "Mrs. Cummings?"

Avery's mother was already pushing her way up from the center of the crowd. They all went back inside the building, and Mrs. Cummings hugged both Avery and Jere fiercely. The police officer escorted them up to the Cummingses' apartment.

Jere called his mother to tell her what had happened. One of the officers took the phone after he was finished and said he would give Jere a ride home as soon as they were done. Or, if they wanted to see their son immediately, they could come over and be admitted to the building. "Yes, ma'am, all right, I'd do that, too, if it was my boy. We'll be waiting for you at the back entrance."

Officer Bradley came in a few minutes later. "It's over now," she said. "Al Watkins died on the way to the hospital. Our officers tried not to kill him, but he was shooting and moving in close quarters. They wanted to protect you, Jere, and they were under fire themselves."

Avery burst into tears again. Her mother put her arm around her on one side and Officer Bradley put her arm around her on the other. "We have people you can talk to about this. You too, Jere. This is a rough experience."

Jere still felt numb.

In a short time, his mother and father were at the Cummingses' door, his mother hugging him without a word. His father stood to the side, then shook Officer Bradley's hand.

"We wouldn't have wanted it to end this way, but where guns are involved, it's always a risk," said Officer Bradley. "When the officers called in code forty-seven, we knew this was a possibility. Code forty-seven means ongoing situation with live gun, immediate danger, send help."

Jere and Avery talked to the police for nearly an hour, coming up with as many details as they could. The police officers said Jere and Avery didn't have to go back down to the laundry room right then to show them what had happened, but they might have to later on. "You handled him real well, Jere," said Officer Bradley. "Like a pro. You had good instincts."

Jere nodded. He couldn't remember having had any

instincts whatsoever, except a desire to be out of there.

The police speculated that Watkins had followed Avery, had figured out where she lived, had gained access to the building during the day, and by pure chance had come upon the unused room in the basement. The laundry space had been renovated two years before, and as there had been no use for the cramped little room, it had been ignored ever since.

"When I think of it! He was down there all along!" Avery's mother said. She and Jere's mother clasped each other's hands for a moment.

"One thing we'll do is get in touch with the girl's parents as soon as we can locate them," said Officer Bradley before she left. "Knowing who the killer was and knowing that he's dead may give them some sort of sense of closure."

Jere and Avery agreed to go to the police station the next day to help file a complete report.

"So," said Jere.

"So," said Avery. She touched his arm lightly.

Jere and his parents walked along the corridor to the elevator. He didn't know what he felt as the numbness started to recede. The terror of the basement room threatened to sweep back over him, and he guessed it probably would be a while before he was rid of that. He had felt a moment of terrible and confusing pity when he saw the bird man bloodstained and crumpled on the floor. For a time, he had almost walked in the bird man's shoes; he had lived with him in his dreams. But pity was washed aside by the overwhelming relief of survival.

He was so lucky to be alive! It came over him in a rush—he and Avery both, they were *alive.*

His father must have been holding back his emotion on that score, too, for when they left the building and reached the parking lot, he stopped Jere and wrapped his arms around him and said, "Son," just once, and hugged him tight and long.

Avery threw a handful of grass at Jere. They were lying on their backs on the bank of the pond near school, letting the May sun warm up their arms and legs, soak through their shirts. Someone's dog appeared over Jere's face and panted down at him. Jere smelled doggy breath, and the dog gave his ear a lick before its owner called it sharply away.

"So we're going to Montana for six weeks," Avery said. "My mom's cousin owns this trail-guide place, and we're going to live there and go for hikes and all, and Mom's going to finish her thesis, whatever."

"Six weeks? What do you have to go so long for?"

"Just had the lucky chance. But here's *your* lucky chance. Want to come? They have extra rooms, and they need guys to do stuff like cut away these weeds that grow on the paths, something like that. You can get *paid.* You're not doing anything special this summer, are you?"

"Not much." He had signed up for two weeks of soccer camp, and nothing else was coming up but going swimming and mowing people's lawns.

"That's settled, then. Great! Don't you want to? Do you think your parents will let you? Aunt Diane's going to be there, too. My mom says I really need someone like you to keep me out of trouble."

"She says *what?*"

Avery jumped to her feet and nudged him in the ribs with her toe. "Come on."

They went across the long grass of the school grounds together. Jere lazily stretched his arm across Avery's shoulders, and she reached up and gave him a fleeting kiss on his chin, then pushed him and ran off laughing, daring him to catch up with her—which he did.